Butterflies in May

KAREN HART

bancroft
press

Published by Bancroft Press ("Books that enlighten")
P.O. Box 65360, Baltimore, MD 21209
800-637-7377
410-764-1967 (fax)
www.bancroftpress.com

Cover and interior design: Tammy Sneath Grimes, Crescent Communications
www.tsgcrescent.com • 814.941.7447

Author photo: Gary Greinke

ISBN 1890862-44-4
LCCN 2005931541

Printed in the United States of America

First Edition

1 3 5 7 9 10 8 6 4 2

What may seem our darkest hour may only be as the caterpillar to the butterfly that flies free in spring. The road of a lowly, slow-moving creature seems long compared to the brief burst of beauty that is the butterfly, but it is in the transformation that the real beauty of the butterfly lies.

—Imara

For all who are faced
with an unplanned pregnancy

Chapter 1

Everything in your life can change in a single instant. That occurred to me this morning, when I realized my period was MIA—missing in action. Suddenly, my entire world shifted. The most pressing things on my mind yesterday were a paper I was writing for government class, the realization that I'm an anarchist, and deciding whether to wear that new cropped sweater to school or save it for the football game Friday night. Now all I can think about is this.

It's probably nothing. It *has* to be nothing, but I'm worried. My periods have never been regular. I'm always two or three days late, and once I was even a week late. But this time, I'm ten days late. That's a record.

Still, Matt and I are careful. We don't usually take chances—not like some girls in my class. Last New Year's Eve, my best friend, Monica, had a sleep-over party, and five other girls, including myself, stayed up most of the night talking. One girl, Robin Evans, said she had done it with four different guys and never used protection with any of them. Talk about incredibly stupid.

That was junior year, when I was taking my first journalism class. The thought of being that careless outraged me so much that I wrote a series of articles about teens and sex titled "Get Real." I wrote how we should take responsibility for our actions, and about the success rates of various methods of birth control. Monica read my articles and said I should lighten up, but she thinks I take everything too seriously.

Mrs. Danker, my journalism teacher, said the articles were

"brilliant" and "insightful" and "struck a chord." She even asked my permission to run them in the student paper, *The Voice*. But after the first article "Teens and Sex" appeared, along with a sidebar about abstinence-only education and how students really felt about it, a group of outraged parents went to the school board and demanded that the series stop. One parent said the article was "suggestive," and four others agreed. Then a board member said the article might undercut parental authority and encourage "the children" to have sex. After that, the board voted unanimously to stop the series, as if that would solve anything. Obviously, the authorities here don't realize that when it comes to sex, no one asks their parents for permission first.

Mrs. Danker, who's more enlightened than the parents and board members, tried to save the series, but apparently First Amendment rights don't apply to school newspapers. The rest of the articles were never published, but Mrs. Danker asked if I would be the paper's editor my senior year and write a column each month. I may groan and complain about it—and believe me, I'm not the type of student who complains about everything—but it's empowering to have a voice.

School is out for the day, and I'm making my way down a hallway, past the principal's office and a row of lockers. When I turn the corner, there's Andy leaning against my locker, waiting for me.

"Hey, Parker."

"Hey, yourself." I've known Andy since middle school, but we probably never said more than seven words to each other until we wound up in the same journalism class last year. Andy's got a 4.40 GPA (you get extra points for AP classes) and is bound for some prestigious college, but you'd never guess it from looking at him. Today, he's wearing a rumpled t-shirt and shorts, no socks, and has a candy bar hanging out of his mouth. He's a math brain who, by some quirk of fate, can write clear and sometimes clever copy with hardly any effort at all. Sometimes, I find it annoying.

Sometimes, I'm more than a little envious. But he really is a nice guy, and it's been fun working on articles with him for the paper. Whenever I get frustrated with a column I'm writing or the school board's constant involvement with our paper, I appreciate having a goofball genius like him around.

"About my article . . ." he begins.

I know what this is about. His article for the paper is due tomorrow, but Andy thinks deadlines are for other people, not him. I know for a fact that he missed every single deadline last year.

"Look, I need two more days to finish that article."

"Two? No way."

"Okay . . . one."

"Deal," I say. I know he'll get it to me by then.

"Really?"

"Really."

He smiles, walks backwards, and trips over a garbage can.

Five minutes later, Matt pulls up in his car to give me a ride home. It's a beater, but it has a ragtop and a lot of character. Reaching across the seat to open the door for me, he smiles, which is enough to make me stop worrying, at least for now. There's something about the way he looks at me—as if no other girl on the planet exists. It gets me every time. I climb in beside him, and he gives me a quick kiss before taking off. It's the last week of September, and the leaves are just starting to change, but it still feels like summer—Indian summer. I wish it could last forever.

During the summer, Matt and I had been able to see each other nearly every night. He worked construction, and I worked the afternoon shift at Java House making espresso drinks. But now that he's bagging groceries most nights at Vincent's Market, and I'm working weekends, we have a lot less time to spend with each other.

"Do you think you'll come by later?" I ask, hoping he will. "Aunt Laura's birthday is today, and she's coming up from the city for dinner at my house." He has to work tonight until 8:00.

He glances at me. "Are you sure it's okay?"

What he really wants to know is whether it's okay with my mom. There's always an undeniable chill in the air whenever Matt and Mom are in the same room together. I have no idea why Mom is so cool toward Matt. She's always great with my other friends, but she's different with Matt. I asked her about it once, but she acted like she didn't know what I was talking about. My father rescued her. "Ali, of course your mother likes Matt. We both do," he'd said. Mom stood there, nodding like a maniac with a smile frozen on her face, but I saw the truth. My dad likes Matt. My mother tolerates him—barely.

"Sure. My mom said to invite you," I say, which is not even remotely true.

"Okay," he says. "I'll try."

But I know he won't. He hardly ever stops by when he knows my mother'll be there. We're quiet for a few minutes, and then I remember that Matt had a meeting with his guidance counselor today. "How'd it go with Meyers?"

Almost everyone I know is applying to Illinois universities, except for Matt. His number one choice is Pratt Institute, which is in New York. He likes it for two reasons. One, it has the best fine arts program in the country. And two, he thinks he can get a full scholarship there. I know how important it is for him to get the scholarship at Pratt. Matt's parents earn a decent living, but they have five kids to put through college, so they're strongly encouraging him to apply for scholarship money.

"He thinks my chances of getting a big scholarship are good," Matt says.

"That's great," I say, even though I don't want to think about next year.

Before Matt and I started dating, my number one choice was Northwestern because it's nearby and has an excellent journalism program. But it's more than 800 miles away from Pratt. Last week, I told my mother I also want to apply to Columbia and NYU because they're both in New York. From Columbia, Pratt's only 45 minutes away by subway, and NYU is even closer. Matt and I could see each other a lot, and probably every weekend. My mother had said, "You've always had your heart set on Northwestern, Ali. I don't think you should apply to schools just because they're close to Pratt." But when I pointed out that Columbia and NYU both have strong journalism programs, it was hard for her to argue.

"Okay," she'd finally said. "Go ahead and apply, but I expect you to apply to Northwestern also, the way you've always planned."

Matt pulls over to the side of the street, a couple of houses away from mine, and puts the car in park. He draws me close and kisses me—lightly at first, but then his arms tighten, and the kiss gets hard and deep. Before I leave, I almost tell him my period's late, but I don't want to worry him. I did skip school during lunch to buy a pregnancy kit, which I jammed into my backpack before the clerk had time to put it in a bag for me. It's still there, underneath a copy of *Macbeth* and two spiral notebooks. I'll take the test, find out for sure it's negative, and then stop worrying about it. It has to be negative. I'll be graduating in the spring, and the future is full of endless possibilities. There's college, travel, a job in Chicago, a fabulous apartment, and who knows what else? Only one thing is certain: Matt. All futures include Matt.

I've lived at 207 Camden Street for most of my life. It's your basic, traditional two-story house with shutters and looks like every other house on the street. When people come over the first time, they're usually surprised to see how contemporary it looks inside. Most of the furniture is modern and in neutral colors, but there are a few traditional pieces, and the walls are covered with bright watercolors that my mom picks up at art festivals. And every room is filled with pottery, sculptures, and hand-painted wood boxes—pieces that you'd never think to put together in the same house—but somehow it all works and everyone always comments on how great everything looks.

My mom, Kate Parker, is on the kitchen phone when I walk in the back door. Everyone says I look like my mother. We're both 5' 4" and have fine features and the same blue-green eyes, but our hair is different. Mine is long, dark blonde, and turns lighter in the summer. Mom's hair is the same color, but she keeps it short and highlights it now to cover the gray.

"You're home early," I say when she hangs up.

"I wanted to get a head start on dinner, and the plumber's supposed to stop by to fix the faucet. I didn't know if you'd be home in time to let him in."

"Oh." I lean against the counter and watch her squeeze lime juice into a bowl. A bag of groceries is on the counter, and next to the bowl are limes, a bottle of rosemary-mint shampoo, and raw chicken. Sometimes, I don't want to know what she's concocting, but today, I can't help myself. The shampoo makes me nervous. "What are you making?"

"Lime-pepper marinade . . . for chicken. But I got you tofu."

"Thanks," I say, grabbing a can of pop from the refrigerator. I gave up meat this summer after watching a documentary on how animals are butchered. It grossed me out, and now my mother is abnormally preoccupied with protein. She thinks I'm not getting enough of it.

She hands me the shampoo. "For you," she says. *(Thank God it's not part of the marinade.)*

"Oh, yeah," I say. "I invited Matt to stop by after work." I hold my breath, waiting for her reaction.

My mother doesn't bother to look up. She shakes some salt into the marinade and says, "Oh," as if it's the worst idea she's ever heard.

"What time is he coming by?"

"He gets off at 8:00."

She nods distractedly, as if she's completely absorbed by the recipe on the counter. I head upstairs to my room before she can say anything else.

❧

It's no use—I can't focus. I'm sitting at my desk, homework piled high, but all I can think about is the pregnancy kit still in my backpack.

It was easy to forget about on the drive home with Matt. But if I allowed myself, I could easily have a mini-breakdown right now. Fortunately, Monica bursts into my room and saves me.

"I hate my life," Monica announces as she flops down on the bed. This is our daily ritual. After school, either I go to Monica's house or Monica comes here to complain and decompress.

Monica is a drama queen. I think she should major in drama next year in college, but she's not interested. Monica is always changing her look, too. Today, she's wearing moccasins, a tie-dyed shirt-skirt combo, and hair beads. I've heard what the girls at school say about her. They think she's a flake. But the truth is, Monica is the most grounded person I know.

"What's up?" I ask, knowing this latest drama probably has something to do with her new stepdad. Monica's mom remarried over the summer. Steve Marsac seems like the typical friendly, balding, overamped stepfather. I actually like him—he was a relief after the string of losers Monica's mom dated the past three years—but Monica despises him. She's suspicious of anyone who tries too hard to win her over. I think she should give her stepdad a chance, but out of loyalty, I keep my thoughts to myself.

"First," she says, "Steve has decided to play guidance counselor and wants to spend this weekend going over college brochures with me. And second, Kyle is coming home for the weekend, which means every night will be family night in my mother's ongoing quest to turn us into one cohesive family." Monica rolls onto her back and groans at the ceiling. "You're so *lucky* your parents aren't divorced."

"What's wrong with Kyle?" I ask. He's Monica's new step-brother. He'd been living with his mom in California until a month ago. I met him briefly at the wedding this summer. He has a great body and nice teeth. Monica usually goes for guys like that, but he is her stepbrother, and like me, she's never had to deal with a sibling. This year, Kyle's a freshman at Northwestern, so he'll be spending occasional weekends at Monica's house.

"Oh, *pleeeease*. For one, he's constantly bragging about how he's making it with all these college women, which I don't believe for a minute. Two, he thinks my outfits are goofy, so he assumes I'm incapable of a complete thought. Three . . . never mind." She takes a deep breath and exhales loudly. "I saw Niles today . . . with Robin Evans."

Niles Sherman is a friend of Matt. They met this summer when Niles got a job working for the same construction company as Matt. They started hanging out together, which is how Niles and Monica hooked up. Niles is wild and different and reckless. He always talks about parties he goes to where the cops show up, and about the road trips he takes. And he drives like a maniac. His driver's license was suspended last month after he got a speeding ticket for going 95 mph. He still drives anyway.

When Monica first met Niles, she was fascinated with him, but Niles isn't the sort of guy who stays with one girl for long. This summer, he would unexpectedly show up at Monica's house, but he never knocked on the front door. Instead, he'd throw a pebble at her window to get her attention. She'd sneak out of the house, and they'd go driving around.

But that all changed when school started. Now, suddenly, Niles and Robin Evans are always together. I know it bothers Monica, though she pretends it doesn't. Monica is usually the first to move on in a relationship, but this time Niles is the one who called it quits. He's stopped showing up at her house.

Monica shrugs. "It's not like I liked him that much anyway," she says. "Besides, I want to go out with someone older and more experienced and—"

"Experienced?"

"You know . . ." Monica makes a "V" sign with her fingers. "I think I'm the only one in our class. I definitely don't want to start college that way."

"That's a *great* reason," I say, sarcastically.

"Well, not everyone can be going out with Mr. Perfect, Ali."

I roll my eyes.

"See, you can't even deny it because you know it's true."

It *is* true. Actually, Monica introduced me to Matt, which is amazing when you think about it. Monica is really beautiful, with long dark hair and a perfect body. Most guys fall for her immediately, but Matt seems completely oblivious to her. He's never shown any interest in her at all other than being her friend. Matt started going to our high school last February when his family moved here from Ohio. It might have been tragic for most people, moving in the middle of high school like that, but Matt had two things going for him. A) He was tall and gorgeous. B) He was new, so everyone was intrigued.

The cheerleaders swarmed him immediately. Sarah Vogel (head cheerleader, queen bee) followed him around like a puppy for weeks, introducing him to all the cheerleaders and the rest of her entourage. The jocks liked him because he was a natural athlete, but he was no threat to them because he wasn't interested in joining a team. But it didn't look like he fit it in with that crowd of cheerleaders and jocks, and he was just as likely to eat with the science geeks or the math nerds or even someone like me, which is how I met him.

He and Monica had been in the same P.E. class. One day at lunch, he set his tray on our table and asked Monica if he could join us. He was wearing a black t-shirt—it had a peace sign on the front—and a baseball cap, which he wore backwards. He had straight dark hair and deep blue eyes that reminded me of the ocean after a storm. At first, I thought he was interested in Monica, because most guys usually are, but he kept watching me all through lunch and asking me questions—even Monica noticed. A week later, he gave me a ride home from school and asked if he could sketch me for his advanced art class. They were doing portraits, and he said I had an interesting face. I didn't know if that was good or bad, but I liked the way I felt whenever he looked at me.

He sketched me the next day after school, and then he started looking for me every day at lunch. My life began to revolve around lunch period. I noticed, for instance, that he never drank pop ("toxic," he said), and he favored t-shirts that bore some message like "Save the Rainforests," "Recycle," or "Think Peace." Suddenly, the world seemed brighter, and I knew I was starting to fall for him. I loved how I felt when I was with him. I had never felt this way before. Then, one day between classes, he was waiting for me by my locker.

"You like me," he said.

"What makes you think that?"

"Because of this." And just as the warning bell rang, he leaned in and kissed me, fast, before I could react.

A week later, we were driving around in his car, talking and laughing and listening to the radio under a bright blue sky. I showed him the way to Willow Lake. We took off our shoes and walked along the water's edge, just playing around, when he put his arms around me and pulled me close. He kissed me and smoothed my hair. I closed my eyes and felt it for the first time—that rush you feel when you're with someone you really care about. I kissed him back, and I felt different somehow, as if I'd crossed some threshold, as if he was about to lead me somewhere new.

Before, with other guys, I was always happy with kissing and holding hands, but for the first time ever, I found myself wanting more. The thing is, I never had a definite timeline. I wanted to take my time, not have it happen in some mad rush or in the backseat of a car with some random guy. The other reason I waited was because, frankly, there was no one I even wanted to go there with. When I lost my virginity, I wanted it to be meaningful. I've heard how some of the guys talk about the girls they've been with, rating each of them on a scale of one to ten. Then they laugh among themselves about some of the girls. I don't even want to imagine what the guys say about those girls.

I knew Matt had experience, and he knew I was a virgin because he had asked. We took it slowly because I wasn't ready. The truth is, I was scared. Then, on June twenty-first, the first day of summer, we went to Willow Lake with Monica and Niles. We played volleyball for a while, and Monica took some pictures. After lunch, Monica and Niles took off, leaving me and Matt alone— swimming and laughing. The sky was wide and blue, and the sun was shining. We were in the center of the lake's shallow end, splashing and playing around, when he got serious.

"There's something I've been meaning to tell you," he said.

I thought he was goofing around, so I splashed him. "What?" I asked.

He took my hand and pulled me close. "I'm being serious here." He smelled like suntan lotion and lake water.

"Okay," I said. "Me, too."

"I love you," he said—just like that. And the way he looked at me, I knew he wasn't kidding around.

I didn't say it back right away, even though I wanted to, even though I'd been thinking the same thing for weeks. My throat closed and I got tears in my eyes, and I hoped he knew I felt the same way. Later, when the sky was turning orange and red, he said he wanted to be alone with me, and I knew why. We went for a walk, bringing a blanket with us. We found a place by a tree, far away from the rest of the world. We were lying there on the ground, fooling around like we had been lately, but this time I didn't want him to stop. We kept going, and it felt so good. I couldn't get close enough to him. I couldn't say why exactly.

Maybe it was the color of the sky or the way he asked if I was really sure. But I was seventeen years old, I loved him, and I knew I was ready. We had known each other exactly three months and 21 days.

Afterwards, I said, "I love you, too."

"I know," he said and pulled me close.

I can't imagine doing something that intimate with someone I didn't love. I'm glad I waited, and I'm glad it was with Matt. But I know some girls will casually hook up with any guy, and I hope Monica doesn't become one of them just to get the experience.

I look at Monica, who's still sprawled on my bed. "Do you have a *timeline* now?" I ask. "Don't be in such a hurry," I add, thinking about the pregnancy kit in my backpack. "Mon . . ." I almost tell her I'm late. After all, she's my best friend. "What?"

I shake my head. "Nothing."

Monica glances at the alarm clock on my nightstand. "I gotta go. I promised my mom I'd be home half an hour ago. Did you remember to bring home your notes?"

"Yeah. They're in my backpack." The phone on my desk rings, so I pick it up. Last year, I begged my parents for my own private line. They vetoed the idea, but at least they ran an extension into my room. "Hello?"

Monica mumbles something to me, but the connection is so bad I turn my back to her and use a finger to plug my other ear. "Hello?" I say again. Whoever it is must be calling from a cell phone. Through all the static, all I can make out is that it's the plumber. He promises to call right back. I hang up and am about to get my notes on *Macbeth*, but Monica is already rummaging through my backpack.

"Monica . . . wait," I say, trying to sound more casual than I feel. But it's too late. Monica is holding the pregnancy kit.

"Oh, my God . . . Ali? Are you . . . ?"

Chapter 2

"Don't say it. Don't even *think* it. Besides, I'm not. In fact, I'm sure I'm not." The phone rings again, but I ignore it. It's probably the plumber calling back.

"Then what's this for?" Monica asks, waving the box at me.

"It's nothing, okay? I'm a little late . . . I just want to be sure."

I grab the box from her and slip it in a drawer under a sweater.

"How late *are* you?"

"Ten days."

"*Ten days?!*"

"Look, I've never been regular—you know that." I can hear my mom downstairs talking to the plumber on the phone.

"Still, ten days is . . . substantial." Monica sits on my bed, crossing her legs under her. Obviously, she's no longer in a hurry to get home. "*OhmyGod*, Ali . . . I thought you guys were careful."

"We *are* careful," I say, which is true. But there *had* been one time . . . I try not to think of it. "Well, most of the time."

"*OhmyGod*," she says again, her voice a whisper, as if it's happening to her.

I go over and sit beside her on the bed, trying to look like this is really no big deal. We've spent a lifetime within these lavender walls, on the floral bedspread my mom picked out for me when I was still in elementary school. Monica and I have talked about everything in this room, but never anything like this. I lean against the headboard, pulling my legs against my chest. The doorbell rings, and I hear my mother open the front door to let the plumber in.

Monica glances over at me. "Does Matt know?"

"No, it just occurred to me this morning. Besides, I've been late before, so there's nothing to tell. I got the test just to be sure. If the result is, you know, then . . ." I can't even finish the thought. It's not that I'm superstitious, but now I feel as if saying the word "positive" would jinx everything. Can you cause something to happen just by thinking it? Sometimes I think so.

When she recovers from the shock, Monica immediately takes charge. "Do you want me to stay while you take the test?" she asks, reaching out to touch my arm.

"No. It's okay."

Monica and I have been best friends forever. This is the girl who suffered through years of summer camp with me, who taught me how to use a tampon and apply eye shadow, who understands about Matt, and who believes I've got real talent as a writer. We've been through everything together, but I want to be alone when I take the test. Besides, I'm not entirely ready to deal with it just yet. "I don't have time now anyway. I'll take it later."

"Are you going to be okay? I hate leaving you like this, but Mom will come unglued if I don't get home soon."

"I'm fine—really."

Not until after she pulls out of the driveway do I realize she'd forgotten to take my *Macbeth* notes.

⟡

I'm using a fork to push the cake around on my plate. It's my favorite—chocolate cake with raspberry filling and butter cream frosting—but tonight it doesn't taste good to me. The possibility of being pregnant—no matter how slim—is making me sick. I feel like I'm moving through water, drowning in murky green waves right in front of my family, but no one notices.

My mother is talking about some art exhibit, but I hardly hear her. All I can think about is whether or not I'm pregnant. I don't feel any different. My breasts are slightly bigger, and my stomach feels a little bloated, but that always happens right before I get my period.

"Ali?"

I blink as my mother leans forward in her chair. "Did you hear me? I was asking if you want to come with us to the art exhibit this weekend. It's in the city. Aunt Laura's going to meet us there."

"I have to work and I have a paper to write," I say, which is my standard line whenever my mother wants me to do something I don't want to do. My dad kicks me under the table. If *he's* going, *I'm* going. "Well . . . maybe," I say, shooting him a look.

"Are you feeling okay?" Dad asks, peering over his bifocals. "You usually devour two pieces of this stuff at one sitting."

"Just because I'm not eating like a truck driver doesn't mean I'm sick." We all laugh, and already I feel a little better. It's so like my dad to notice. He's the nicest man I know. Yesterday, I saw him talking to our neighbor's golden retriever on the back porch, and I swear that dog listened.

"I remember my appetite dropping off when I was Ali's age," Aunt Laura chimes in. "It's a good thing, too, or I'd look like a beach ball."

That's hard to imagine. Aunt Laura is petite—she can't weigh more than a hundred pounds. But she's much tougher than she looks. According to Mom, Aunt Laura is the rising star at the ad agency because she's tough as nails.

"So, how's senior year going?" Aunt Laura asks.

"Great," I say, trying not to think about the pregnancy kit upstairs.

"It's such an exciting time in your life—winding up that last year in high school, applying to schools, visiting college campuses," she says, running a hand through her auburn hair, which hangs to her shoulders.

She has a faraway look in her eyes. "My senior year, I was in love with Tommy Brown, but he didn't know I existed."

"Really?" It's hard to imagine. Aunt Laura has no problem finding men to date.

"Yes, I was painfully shy and a late bloomer. He was out of my league . . . I wonder what ever happened to him?" She shakes her head as if to bring herself back to the present, and looks closely at me. "But look at you. You're positively glowing. You must still be seeing Matt."

"Where is Matt tonight?" Dad asks. "I thought he was stopping by."

"He's working, but he may stop by later."

"He's a great kid," Dad says.

"And cute," Aunt Laura says, winking at me.

Mom stands up, her nose slightly wrinkled. She begins to clear the plates. "Laura, did Ali tell you she's editor of the school paper this year?" Mom smiles—a fake smile. Typical. She always manages to change the subject whenever Matt's name comes up.

"Yes, she did," Aunt Laura says.

"Where's Matt applying to college?" Dad asks, completely oblivious to my mother.

I watch as she leaves the room. "Pratt Institute, The School of the Art Institute of Chicago, and the University of Illinois."

"All fine schools," Dad says.

Dad and I start clearing the table. He's in pharmaceutical sales and travels a lot on business, but when he's home for dinner, we always clear the table together.

Aunt Laura glances at her watch. "I need to cut out early," she says. "I have an early meeting tomorrow." Aunt Laura lives in a high-rise apartment in Chicago, along Lake Shore Drive. Depending on traffic, it's about an hour's drive from Lakeview. "Thanks for the great party, guys." She hugs me, then Mom.

"So how old *are* you, Aunt Laura?" I ask, right before she

leaves.

"Thirty-eight. It probably sounds like a hundred to you, kid-do, but trust me, those years creep up fast." She sighs. "And, you know, my biological clock is ticking louder and louder. In fact, it's keeping me up at night."

"You still have plenty of time to find someone special and start a family," Mom says.

Aunt Laura sighs. "I hope you're right."

My aunt gives me a squeeze before I head upstairs. All I can think about is the pregnancy kit in my room.

⤫

Take any time. Results in three minutes. 99% accurate.

It looked like the easiest test in the pharmacy, which was why I bought it. I open the box and read the sheet of instructions. According to the directions, it's practically idiot proof. I can take the test right now and find out one way or another in just three minutes. Once I know for certain, I can stop obsessing about being late.

The phone rings while I'm looking for somewhere to hide the kit, just in case I run into Mom or Dad on the way to the bath-room. I check the clock on my nightstand. It's 10:30, which means the call's probably for me—no one calls my parents this late.

"Hello?"

"Hi." It's Matt. "Hey, I'm sorry I didn't stop by, but . . ."

"It's okay." I find a bath towel crumpled up on the floor, fold it into a neat square, and hide the pregnancy kit between the folds. My parents respect my privacy, but sometimes they tap once on the door and walk in. The last thing I want is for them to catch me off-guard with this.

"I wanted to talk to you about something," Matt says.

"What?" Something in his voice stops me. He sounds so se-rious. A million thoughts come to mind—he wants to see other people, he wants to break up. Things are so perfect between us that sometimes I think it can't possibly last.

"I don't know . . ."

"Whatever it is, Matt, just say it."

"Well, you were so quiet in the car today, and I've been thinking about it all night. I don't want to sound, you know, egocentric, but I know I've been talking non-stop about going to Pratt next year—assuming I get in—and I know your mom's not happy about you applying to Columbia and NYU, but I was thinking . . ."

I smile. "It's not that."

"Then what?"

I'd promised myself I wouldn't say anything to Matt until I knew for sure, but I can't keep it from him. "I haven't gotten my period yet. I'm a little worried about it."

He doesn't say anything. "Look, it's probably nothing," I say, as if I know what I'm talking about—as if I'm not worried about it at all.

"You think?"

"Yeah. I mean, I'm always late." I shrug it off. "I'm sure I'll get it in a few days." *Why did I have to tell him over the phone?*

"Good." He sounds relieved, as if it's already a done deal. "Hey, Ali?"

"Yeah?"

"I love you."

"I love you, too." I hang up and look at the towel in my lap. I think about taking the pregnancy test, but decide not to. There's no way I'm pregnant—that's something that happens to other girls. I'm probably late only because I'm worrying about it so much. I read something about that in a magazine once. I decide to stop obsessing—as if it's that simple.

❧

I bury the kit in the bottom of my dresser drawer and try to forget all about it. I go to classes as usual, take a test in government on Thursday, edit the school paper, which is due out on Friday, and laugh at Matt's inane jokes during lunch period, which we nearly always spend together. I've practically forgotten all about it, except when Monica asks me twice whether I've taken the test. Twice I tell her "no." I decide that Monica is a real nag. I'm sure my period will start any day now. It has to.

Then, one morning between classes, I'm using the restroom, and I notice a few drops of blood on my underwear. I'm so relieved. I tell Monica first because she's waiting for me outside the restroom. Monica shrieks and gives me an extra hard hug. When I tell Matt in study hall, he says "cool" and gives me a high five, then laughs when I tell him he's never coming near me again without a condom. That's when I decide to make an appointment at Planned Parenthood and get on the Pill. I don't ever want to go through this again! Later, I worry a little because my period was so light, but I *did* get my period. And by the end of the week, I've already forgotten about this whole business of being late.

Chapter 3

About 800 students go to Lakeview High. We fall into three basic categories. A) Those who are here to get an education and a high school degree, B) Those who are here to prepare for college, and C) Those who are just marking time. From there, we fall into subcultures. There are the Jocks, the Cheerleaders, the Stoners, the Brains, the Partyers, the Thespians, the Goths, and the Geeks. Some people don't fit into any of these subcultures—people like Monica and me.

Monica and I make an unlikely pair, but somehow we've never grown apart. Monica is fun, strong, and loyal. She's not the kind of girl who would go out with your ex-crush or talk about you behind your back. We met in fourth grade when she moved into a house on Bryden Lane, six blocks away from me. We sat next to each other that year in Miss Pierpont's class, and even then, most of the girls hated her. Monica is flat-out gorgeous. She has full lips, long dark hair, and the kind of body that guys notice immediately. Her looks never bothered me, but other girls are either jealous or intimidated by them. As for the guys, they really go for Monica, and over the years, she's acquired a reputation built more on gossip and speculation than on truth. This is partly due to the fact that Monica goes out with a lot of boys. She has this master list of all the boys in her life with whom she's been more than just friends. Niles was number 15. A lot of the kids at school think Monica sleeps around, but in fact she's still a virgin.

My classes this semester aren't that exciting. Government class is a bore. Ditto for business. P.E. is a necessary evil, unless we play volleyball. Journalism is the only class that's even remotely interesting. This year, Monica and I have one class together—first period AP English. Niles Sherman is in that class, too, which proves that you can never know anyone completely. I never would have taken Niles for the school type. I've never seen him with a backpack—he usually carries a notebook and has to borrow a pen. But in AP English, he aced the first pop quiz when everyone else bombed it. Our teacher is an older, bird-like woman with wild, frizzy orange hair. Her name is Mrs. Frye, but everyone calls her Carrot Top. (Not to her face, of course.) Monica thinks she dyes her hair, but it's hard to imagine anyone actually paying money for that color.

Carrot Top is a freak about Shakespeare. She talks about bardolatry and makes air quotes whenever she says that word. "Bardolatry," she says, "is simply a fancy word for 'the worship of Shakespeare.'" (More air quotes.) Niles raises his hand one day and tells Carrot Top she can stop making air quotes. "We get it," he says.

Carrot Top begins every class with a sort of pep talk/sermon. "We owe Shakespeare everything," she says passionately. "He taught us to understand the human experience." She often refers to a thick, well-worn book written by an expert, and it's all about Shakespeare and his plays. She reads excerpts from it and waves it around like it's a sacred text. I wonder if Carrot Top is a "bardolatrist," if there is such a word.

Carrot Top, who loves words as much as Shakespeare did, challenges everyone to bring in a new word once a week so we can build our vocabularies. You get extra credit if you find a word she doesn't already know. So far this year, no one has bothered. She also has us write in our journals every day, so we can "find our souls" (a direct quote, I swear). She promises not to read our journals. I usually stick to safe topics, but Monica writes about Carrot Top. Her hair is a recurring subject.

✎

By the middle of October, my period is due again. I have wicked PMS, my breasts feel sore, and for the first time ever, I'm actually looking forward to having my period. I hope it comes in a flood. One morning, I'm certain I'm having cramps. I go to the bathroom right after my first class, only to find out that my period hasn't started. I can't believe it. I wait a day . . . another . . . and another.

On Friday, I'm officially five days late and starting to panic. I sit through classes the rest of the day, mechanically taking notes, but all I can think is, *what if* . . .

We've always been careful, except for that one time. We'd been messing around, and Matt didn't have a condom. We hadn't planned to actually do anything, but one thing led to another, and we got carried away. It felt so good to do it without a condom. And right before Matt came, he pulled out. I worried at first, but Matt convinced me there was no way I could get pregnant. It was easy to rationalize. In sex ed, they say you can only conceive one week out of a month. So what are the chances? I think about that the rest of the day, and watch the clock in each of my classes as if my life depends on it. When the final bell rings, I'm out of there. Matt gives me a lift home on his way to work, and I hope my parents aren't home yet. There's no way I'm taking a pregnancy test while they're around.

When Matt pulls into the driveway, the garage door is down, which means my parents are still at work. I'd been quiet all the way home, but Matt didn't notice. I think about telling him I'm late again, but then I decide to wait until after I've taken the test. I lean over to kiss him goodbye, and he promises to call later.

I find the pregnancy kit I bought last month and lock myself in the upstairs bathroom. It's so quiet I can hear my heart hammering in my chest. I follow the instructions, but worry I'll make some mistake. Then I clock the time on my wristwatch and do something I haven't done in a long time. I say a prayer, though it's quick and to the point and comes out in a whisper. *"Please, God, not me. Not now."*

According to the instructions, if the test window shows a blue line within three minutes, I'm pregnant. But the guessing game is over in two minutes. The line is so blue, there's no doubt. *Crap!* I stand there completely still. I'm so scared I can't breathe. It's hard to believe this is actually happening to me: Allison Marie Parker, the girl with the 3.8 grade point average, who always does the right thing, and who always takes the safest route.

I stare at the test stick and will the blue line to disappear. No luck. It remains stubbornly there. I head straight to my bedroom and sit on the edge of my bed. I guess I should start crying. If this was happening to Monica, she definitely would. Monica would throw herself on the bed and wail until oblivion. I study my reflection in the mirror on my dresser. My reflection stares back. *Do something*, it says. *Cry. Scream. Wail.* But I can't. *Okay, then call Monica.*

I pick up the phone and punch out her number. Monica answers on the third ring, and I ask her to come over. "Hurry," I say. "It's an emergency." All things considered, I'm remarkably calm.

When Monica gets here, I show her the test stick with the stubborn blue line that refuses to disappear.

"I'm pregnant," I say, but it's hard to believe it's true.

"You can't be. You just had your period."

"No, I'm late again."

She looks at me for a minute. "Maybe the test's wrong."

Monica grabs the pregnancy kit box from my dresser top and reads the instructions. "It says here you could get a false result if you're taking certain drugs or have a rare medical condition."

"I wish I had a rare medical condition."

It's not funny, but we're both so nervous, we sort of laugh. Then we both get quiet, and I start biting my thumbnail, something I haven't done since I was thirteen.

"Weren't you on some drug last month when you had strep throat?"

Monica asks.

"Yeah, but I finished that weeks ago."

"Well . . . maybe it's still in your system. It says some drugs interfere with the test and could cause a false result."

"It also says on the box that this test is *99 percent* accurate."

"Look, let's not worry about this right now," Monica says. "Maybe it's wrong. Go to a doctor and get a *real* pregnancy test done. I'll go with you if you want. Your parents don't have to know a thing." Monica sits on the bed next to me. "Does Matt know?"

"No." I shake my head. He's still at work, and besides, I don't think I could handle telling him now. I finally start crying, and Monica gives me a hug. All my life, I thought destiny was like a lump of clay—something you mold however you want, and something that always works in your favor. All this time, I was so sure I wasn't pregnant. But maybe I've been kidding myself. These last few weeks, I've been feeling a little sick in the mornings, but I didn't think anything of it. And my period last month—it was practically nonexistent.

"Okay," I finally say. "I'll go to the clinic for a test." I have this terrible feeling, but I hope Monica's right. Maybe the test is wrong. Maybe it's old or defective or I goofed it up.

<hr />

The nightmare continues into the weekend. Everything is wrong. I wake up Saturday with a headache. The sky is gray, and it looks like it's freezing outside. I try calling Planned Parenthood first thing, but I get lost in voice mail hell. Then I'm on hold, waiting to speak to a counselor about an abortion, when I hear a knock on my bedroom door. I hang up fast.

"Are you up?" asks my mother, barging right in. "It's after 10:00, and I thought you were working today."

"I am, but I don't have to be there until 11:30," I say, pretending to yawn and stretch. I try not to look at her directly.

I shower and then try calling Planned Parenthood again, but I get put on hold once more, and after a few minutes, I hang up. I didn't realize they were that busy. I don't have time to call later today because of work, and the clinic's probably closed Sunday, so I'll have to wait until Monday to make the appointment.

When I go downstairs for breakfast, my mother's at the kitchen table, and I can tell she has something to say. The air feels heavy and charged.

"Hi," I say.

"Good morning, Ali," Mom says very stiffly. "Good morning" is not the sort of thing she usually says. I pour myself a bowl of corn flakes while Mom refills her coffee mug. Mom is a weekend artist of sorts—she usually spends Saturday mornings in her studio painting. But today, she sits there reading the paper, glancing up now and then to look at me.

I want to ask Mom what's up, but stop myself. Something tells me I don't want to know what the matter is. *God, what if she heard me calling Planned Parenthood?*

I'm almost finished with my cereal when Mom says, "Ali, I think you're spending too much time with Matt. You're too young to tie yourself down with one boy."

All of a sudden, the corn flakes stick in my throat. I swallow hard.

"How can you say that? Matt works nearly every night. We hardly see each other any more."

"Ali . . . you know what I mean."

"Are you telling me not to see him?"

"Don't be so dramatic. Of *course* not. I just think you should expand your world. Go out more with your friends, like you used to . . . Meet new people," she says, as if this is something she just thought up—as if she hasn't been rehearsing it in her head all morning.

I take my bowl to the sink and dump the rest of my cereal down the disposal. Here I am, pregnant, and my mother's concerned I'm not meeting new people. It's laughable—it really is. I'm not sure what to say, so I do what always works best. I change the subject. Maybe she'll take the hint.

"May I borrow your car?" I ask.

"Sure," she says.

I turn to leave.

"Ali . . . just think about what I said. Okay?"

"Sure." *Whatever* . . . My mother's concern that I'm spending too much time with Matt is the least of my problems now.

The rest of the weekend moves by in slow motion. I'm not sure what to do. Have the baby? I'm going to college next year—there's no room in my life for a baby. Besides, my parents would flip out. I'm pretty sure they still think I'm a virgin. Mom had "the talk" with me when I was ten, and then again when I started dating because of the whole AIDS issue. When Matt and I started spending a lot of time together, she brought it up again.

"Mom, I'm not . . . we're not . . ."

"Oh," she said, visibly relieved.

"Well, if you ever want to talk . . ."

"Sure," I said. "Thanks."

A few days after that conversation, Mom left a brochure for me in my room, *Straight Talk about Sex*. At first, I was mad. Didn't I tell her we weren't doing anything? But when I read it, it was very informative.

The take-home point was that abstinence is the best method of birth control. I know, logically, that makes sense, but I think you have to be realistic. In real life, when you love someone, it's not so easy to keep saying "no." We would have been fine, too, except for that one time. *One time*—I still can't believe it. I wish I had a time machine. Because if I did, I'd go back to that day and do things differently.

For about thirty seconds, I consider telling my parents that I'm pregnant. Then my brain assures me there's no point. It would only upset them, and besides, I've already made up my mind. It'd be too hard to have a baby. Matt and I are only seventeen years old. It's not as if we could keep it. We still have our own lives. And the thing about adoption is that there's no way I can carry a baby for nine months and then give it up and never see it again.

Abortion is the only way. But to be honest, whenever I think about it, I get this awful feeling deep inside. Sure, I'm a pro-choice girl. I've debated abortion in speech classes, and even wrote a paper about it. But now that I'm actually faced with the decision, it's a whole different matter. It doesn't feel right.

My heart points out that this is a baby—a human life—but my brain quickly takes charge. Abortion's easy to rationalize. It's not a baby—it's just a microscopic dot, a tiny dab of protoplasm that can easily go away. I can't wait for the weekend to end. All I want is to make an appointment at the clinic and get it over with.

I hardly talk with Matt all weekend because he's so busy. He took on extra shifts at Vincent's to make extra money. I know I should probably tell him, but I keep thinking that maybe Monica is right. Maybe the test was wrong. Maybe I goofed it up or it was defective. Anything is possible. Then Matt calls between shifts on Saturday and tells me his grandfather in Wisconsin just had a mild heart attack and is in the hospital. I can tell he's upset, so I figure I'll wait to tell him. It's definitely not the right time.

⁂

I call Planned Parenthood on Monday, after first period. The receptionist can squeeze me in that afternoon, if I want. But that won't work because their office is in Chicago, and there's no way I can get there in time. They have an opening on Friday, which is perfect, because there's no school that day. It's Teachers' Institute Day. I make an appointment for Friday morning at 10:30. Monica offers to go with me, so we tell our parents we're going into the city to shop, which we do once or twice a year anyway.

On Friday, Monica picks me up, and we take the train from Lakeview into the city. We find a cab right away and take it to 1200 North LaSalle. The receptionist is an older woman who looks about a hundred. She has long gray hair and is wearing a purple sweater with beads. Her nametag says "Dorothy," but I think of her as Ancient Wise Woman. She asks me to sign in, then hands me a clipboard with some forms to fill out. I wonder if Ancient Wise Woman was sexually active as a teenager. Then I decide that she must have been, otherwise she wouldn't work here.

Monica sits beside me in the reception area while I fill out the forms. On the way to the city, I was fine, but now that I'm actually here, I feel nervous. My hands are damp, and I'm so jittery I can barely hold onto the pen. I glance up, and Ancient Wise Woman looks directly at me and smiles. That helps a little.

I sign a consent form for the pregnancy test and complete a short questionnaire about the first day of my last period, the current form of birth control I'm using, and whether I'm experiencing any nausea, breast tenderness, or other pregnancy symptoms.

When I return the forms to Ancient Wise Woman, I see a girl from school on the other side of the room, a senior named Kelly something. I don't know her, but I've seen her around. Just then, Kelly looks up and our eyes meet, but neither of us says anything.

A few minutes later, a counselor appears and calls my name. She introduces herself as Debby Davis, then leads me to her office at the end of a hall. She's young and pretty, with short brown hair and a nice smile. The office is bright and sunny. There's a poster on the wall showing the female reproductive system, and a large, red geranium on a table near the window. Debby waves me to the chair beside her desk.

She asks where I go to school and a few other general questions. Then she looks over the forms and says, "I understand you're here for a pregnancy test."

"Yes," I say.

"Before we get a specimen, I want to talk with you a bit and give you some information to look over," Debby says. "Have you taken a home pregnancy test?"

"Yes."

"And the results were positive?"

"Are those tests usually accurate?" I say. (*Please, please, please* say no.)

"Usually . . . yes, but we'll check to make sure in a few minutes."

Debby leans forward in her chair. She looks concerned. "How do you feel about the possibility of being pregnant?" she asks.

"I'm only seventeen . . ." I can feel the tears coming on and my throat closes. I shake my head.

"So this was unintended."

I nod. "If I'm pregnant . . . I want an abortion," I finally manage to say. My face is on fire.

Debby doesn't say anything right away. "My job is to make sure you're aware of all the options and have the information you need to make the best decision," she says, handing me a brochure—*What if You're Pregnant?* "You may want to read this while you're waiting for the test results. Do you have a boyfriend?"

"Yes."

"What does he think?"

"I haven't told him."

"Were you planning to wait until after you find out the results of your test?" the counselor asks.

"Yes," I say, thinking I'll tell Matt eventually, but it's hard to believe this is actually happening, and I'm still hoping it's all some crazy mistake.

Debby nods. "Okay," she says. "Now we'll need a specimen from you for the test. I'll take you back to the lab." She stands up. "We'll talk again after we have the results."

Twenty minutes later, a nurse leads me back to the counselor's office. Debby is already at her desk, holding my file in her hands. She's not smiling—not a good sign. As soon as I see her, I know what she's going to say.

"Ali," she says, "the results are positive."

Positive . . . The results are positive. I've known all along, but it's still a shock to hear her say those words. I'm shaking inside and start to cry. Debby hands me a box of tissues and reaches out to touch my arm. I have no idea why I'm acting like this. I've known for days this was possible, but I'd hoped the home pregnancy test had been wrong, that I'd goofed it up or something.

"What about the abortion pill?" I ask. "Is that an option?"

"It may be, depending on how far along you are. When was the first day of your last period?" Debby asks softly.

"August seventeenth . . . I spotted a little in September . . . but it wasn't like a regular period."

"That happens sometimes. And you're right—it's not a regular period." Debby takes out a paper wheel and uses it to show me I'm about nine weeks pregnant. She looks at me for a moment. "I'm afraid it's too late for the abortion pill, but you can have a surgical abortion, if that's what you decide to do."

"Yes," I say in a shaky voice that's a little too loud. "I want to make an appointment now."

"Ali, you mentioned earlier that you haven't told your boyfriend yet. Before making a final decision, you have time to think about what you want to do. Take a few days. Talk with your boyfriend, your parents. Discuss your options with them, too."

I nod my head, as if I'll do exactly that, but I've already considered my options. The thing is, I don't like any of them. "I can't talk with my parents. They'd never understand. Besides, I won't be changing my mind."

"Ali," she says in a careful tone, "don't choose abortion just to keep your parents and your boyfriend from knowing. This is a major decision, one you'll have to live with the rest of your life. Some parents handle it better than you think." For a moment, Debby looks seriously at me. "But if you're certain that's not an option, perhaps you could seek out another adult who can help you through this. Is there a grandparent, a school counselor, or a teacher who could help you?"

"Yeah, I guess so," I say, thinking right away of Aunt Laura. But no, she and Mom talk on the phone nearly every day. Aunt Laura would never agree to keep this a secret from her. Besides, I have Monica and Matt. They're enough. I don't tell the counselor any of this.

Debby seems satisfied. "Good," she says. "Take a few days to think about what feels right to you. The earlier you get serious advice and start looking into your options, the more control you'll have. Then, if you still want to terminate the pregnancy, you can schedule an abortion," says Debby, making a few notes on my chart. "But you really have the time to think this through more thoroughly. You're only nine weeks pregnant, and it's a fairly simple procedure for the first fourteen weeks. After fourteen weeks, the procedure is more complicated."

Debby gives me a packet of information, then talks about the possibility of financial aid and child support if I choose to keep the baby. But I barely hear her. My heart is racing, and I wonder if I'm having a heart attack. Matt's grandfather just had one. Is this possible for someone my age?

Debby continues to go over my options, but the words all float together. "First trimester surgical abortion . . . adoption services . . . prenatal care for the baby." I can't focus on her words. I'm a million miles away, as distant as the stars. Finally, Debby asks, "Are you okay?"

I smile and nod to prove that everything is fine, but I'm not okay at all. Still, I don't totally fall apart the way I half expected to on the way over here this morning. Before I leave, Debby hands me a business card with her name and phone number, and says,

"If you want to talk, call anytime. This is my direct line. I'm here every day. Okay?"

"Sure," I say, taking the card, even though I won't be calling. I've already made up my mind.

Monica is flipping through a magazine in the reception area when I walk in. She looks at me. All I can do is nod.

Monica gives me a hug. "We'll get through this together," she says. Monica stands next to me while I schedule an appointment. Ancient Wise Woman checks my chart and nods when I tell her I need an appointment and why. We set the date for Saturday, two weeks from tomorrow. When she gives me a card with the date of my appointment, Ancient Wise Woman looks at me as if she really understands what I'm going through.

As we head out the door, I notice a mother with her newborn in an infant carrier. The baby is covered with a pink cotton blanket and is fast asleep.

Chapter 4

All weekend I play out a fantasy in my head. It goes something like this: I contract a rare but fatal disease and die. It's something like that movie *A Walk to Remember,* only Matt and I play the starring roles. It's tragic and beautiful and, because I die before anyone finds out I'm pregnant, I don't have to deal with my current situation.

But then I wake up Monday morning, still breathing. I check myself in the bathroom mirror—the picture of health. I hate mornings the most. The reality of what I'm going to do hits me the minute I wake up. I wish I could stop thinking about it.

It's a relief to be back in school. Everything feels normal again. Almost. English—blah, blah, blah. The word of the day is "ambivalence," courtesy of Sarah Vogel. Carrot Top nods approvingly. "Yes, excellent word," she says, writing it on the board, her chalk squeaking all the way. "AM-BIV-A-LENCE . . . It means the existence of mutually conflicting attitudes or feelings, such as love and hate."

No brownie points for Sarah—Carrot Top already knows this word. But I can't stop thinking of it. Next is second period study hall—and Matt. *Ambivalence.* Do I tell him now? Yes. No. I decide to wait. This isn't the sort of thing you whisper in class or write on a note and pass across the aisle.

During lunch, I find Matt with Niles in the school courtyard. Niles is smoking a cigarette, which is "strictly prohibited" on school grounds, but it's the one rule teachers don't bother to enforce unless you're obvious about it.

"Hey, it's Lois Lane," says Niles as soon as he sees me. He started calling me that after the first issue of *The Voice* came out. Then he laughs at his own joke, though it's not that funny or even original, and flicks his cigarette. Matt, sketching Niles, leans against a tree with his sketchpad balanced on his knee. He has to turn in three portraits a week, so he's always looking for someone new to sketch. Matt has real talent. Even Mom, who works with freelance artists all the time, once admitted that his drawings are exceptional. That's quite a compliment, considering how Mom feels about him.

I sit down on the grass and attack my lunch—a hamburger and fries. It's been three months since I've eaten red meat.

"I can't believe you're eating that," Matt says.

"I know."

"Does this mean you're officially a carnivore again?"

"I don't know . . ." As soon as I walked into the cafeteria and smelled the burgers frying, I knew I had to have one. I've already eaten about half of my sandwich when it occurs to me that I was craving red meat. Mom once told me she had craved oranges when she was pregnant with me. I try not to think about it, but it's too late. I can't eat another bite. I set the hamburger back in the paper carton and push it away.

Matt glances at me. "Guilt?"

"Maybe."

"Mind if I finish it?"

"Help yourself."

Matt tosses his sketchbook on a patch of grass. "Thanks, Sherman," he says to Niles, who's writing himself a pass on the pad I saw him swipe off Carrot Top's desk this morning. He can copy any signature perfectly on the first try. At Lakeview, a pink pass is your get-out-of-jail-free card.

"Dude, you wanna skip class?" Niles asks, poised to write Matt a pass. "Pedraza's coming, too." Nick Pedraza hangs out with the burnouts, who spend more time getting stoned in the parking lot than they do in class. I've never had any classes with him, but I see him with Niles a lot.

Matt shakes his head. "Not today . . . I have a trig test."

Before he leaves, Niles picks up the sketchbook, smiling. "Amazing," he says, holding it up. "It looks just like me."

In the picture, Niles has his head resting in the palm of his hand. You can barely see the star tattooed on the inside of his wrist, but there it is. His hair looks a little wilder than usual, and Matt captured the look in his eyes—that slightly wild, reckless look—that Monica found so intriguing.

After Niles leaves, I watch Matt inhale the rest of my lunch while I sit across from him, picking grass blades, and thinking about whether to tell him. It's been on my mind since I took the test at the clinic. In the last six months, Matt has become my clos-est friend, next to Monica. I'm sure he'd want to know. I'm sure he'd think an abortion is the only way out of this mess. The thing is, I don't want to tell him. If I tell him, it makes this nightmare all too real. I don't want to talk about it. I don't want to think about it. Maybe I should just wait until after the abortion to tell him.

"What's wrong?" he asks. "You're so quiet."

"I was just thinking about next year . . . when we start col-lege"—a flat-out lie. "What if I don't get into Columbia or NYU?"

"You will . . . And if you don't, then you'll get into Northwest-ern and we can still see each other."

"Oh, yeah? How's that going to happen?"

"I hear the train is pretty reliable from Chicago to Evan-ston."

"What?"

"I talked with Meyers today, and I asked him about SAIC. Pratt's great and has an outstanding reputation, but SAIC has an excellent art program, too, and it's a lot closer to Northwestern. He thinks I have just as good a chance of getting a scholarship there as at Pratt, though probably not a full one. If I get a scholarship and a loan and keep working part-time, I think I can swing it."

"Wow," I say, "that'd be great."

"Hey, guys," Monica says, walking toward us with a bag of chips and a can of diet pop, her standard lunch when she's dieting. "Mind if I eat with you?"

Matt looks up. "Since when do you have to ask if you can eat with us?"

"I just . . . uh . . . don't want to interrupt you or anything," she says.

"It's okay," I say. "We're just hanging out." I toss Monica a look.

"I gotta run anyway," Matt says. "I've got a trig test next period, and I want to look over my notes."

As soon as he's gone, Monica turns to me. "You didn't tell him, did you?"

"No."

"Ali . . . what are you waiting for?"

"I may not tell him."

"Why not?"

"I don't know. What's the point? I'm having an abortion no matter what. I already made the appointment."

"The point is, he has a right to know," Monica says, slowly enunciating each word, as if I'm deranged.

"I know, Mon, but I just can't." Before, everything was so perfect. So I play this game. As long as I don't talk about it, it isn't real. It's the easiest thing.

I avoid thinking about my next appointment at Planned Parenthood. It's not hard to do. My teachers are in academic mode, pouring on the homework, and Andy and I have been working on a series of articles for *The Voice* about Illinois colleges and how to choose one—a dull but safe topic recommended by the authorities. (They weren't "pleased" with last month's article on fake ID's.)

I keep floating along, pretending it's not really happening. I'm getting really good at it. During the week, I go to classes, work on my articles, and watch trash TV. The only time I really think about it is in the morning when I feel sick to my stomach and when I see the package of unopened tampons stashed in my bathroom drawer. But the weekends are harder. It's Friday afternoon, and I'm in my room, listening to a CD and reading a book. Strike that. *Trying* to read a book. It's no use. I can't focus. I toss the book on my desk and notice the packet of information Debby gave me under a stack of textbooks and folders. I never opened the packet, and now it seems to be screaming at me to take a look. But I already made my decision, so why bother? Abortion is the only way out. I pull out the packet and bury it in my closet under a stack of magazines. Out of sight, out of mind.

I go downstairs for a glass of water and find my mother working at the kitchen table, wearing a thick wool sweater and two pairs of socks. She has a bad cold and spent the day working at home. On the table are a huge mug of tea, a box of tissues, and a pile of black and white photos.

"What are you working on?" I ask, sitting down in the chair next to her.

"It's a brochure for the hospital about our maternity program. I can't decide which photo I like best for the cover. What do *you* think?" she asks, sliding two glossy prints across the table.

Both photographs are good. There's one of a mother holding her baby. The other is a close-up of a baby sleeping. The baby has a fringe of dark lashes that look slightly moist, and tiny, perfect lips.

"I'd go with this one," I say, handing Mom the one of the sleeping baby. "It pulls you in right away." Then, all of a sudden, I feel myself choke up, and I'm certain that if she looks at me closely enough, she'll see the truth.

Instead, Mom smiles, apparently clueless. "I think so, too. Want to help me select the photos for the rest of the brochure?"

I don't have the courage. "Sorry, I can't. I promised Monica I'd come by after school sometime." All of a sudden, I have to get out of the house.

"Will you be home for dinner?"

"Sure," I say, grabbing the denim jacket I left earlier on the kitchen chair.

I let the screen door slam behind me and then hear Mom call, "Dinner's in an hour!"

The air is crisp and smells like wood smoke. I take a deep breath and exhale slowly, then half-run and half-walk to Monica's house. It's only six blocks away. *Just one more week and it'll all be over. Finished. Finito. The End.* But I can't get that photograph of the baby out of my head.

When I get to Monica's house, her mom answers the door. She hyphenated her last name when she remarried this summer, so now she's officially Julie Jacobs-Marsac. I used to call her Mrs. Jacobs, but after the divorce, she insisted I call her Julie. She looks just like Monica, only 30 years older. Today, she's wearing yoga pants with a fuchsia top, and her hair is twisted up in a knot. Julie owns a studio at Lakeview Plaza where she teaches yoga in the mornings and evenings, so I hardly ever see her in normal clothes. She smells like tomato sauce. "Well, hi. Come on in," she says. "I'm in the middle of cooking dinner."

I follow her into the kitchen as she continues talking. "Monica's not here right now. She ran to the store for garlic bread. Want something to drink?"

"Sure, thanks," I say. It's hot in the kitchen. I feel a wave of nausea the minute I step inside. Something's making me feel sick—it's the onions or the garlic. My stomach rumbles. I sit down on a stool near the counter, and she hands me a pop in a juice glass. I take a tentative sip and watch as she chops green peppers.

She asks about my parents and Matt, then starts blabbering about the weather and some cruise she's thinking of taking with Steve, so I nod and smile and hope that if I don't move, the nausea will pass and I can leave. She's talking about her yoga studio and how she's thinking of painting the walls when Kyle comes in the back door, carrying a navy canvas bag over his shoulder.

"Hi," she says. "Kyle, you remember Ali from the wedding, don't you? She's Monica's friend."

"Sure," he says, nodding. "Hi."

"Kyle's home for the weekend to study for a big exam he has on Monday. He's at Northwestern," Julie explains. "I hear you're applying there."

"Yeah." I force a smile. My stomach rumbles again. I don't bother to tell her my new plan that involves Columbia and NYU.

"Maybe you and Monica could drive up some weekend and I'll show you around the campus," he says, helping himself to a can of pop. He takes a swig and leans against the counter. "You okay? No offense or anything, but you don't look so good right now."

I don't bother to answer. All of a sudden, I know I'm going to lose it. I clap a hand over my mouth, rush to the bathroom, and puke in the toilet. A few moments later, there's a knock on the door I didn't have time to close.

"Are you okay?" asks Kyle, walking right in. I'm still kneeling next to the toilet, thinking about the baby in the photograph. Any other time, I'd be mortified to have him in here, but right now, I couldn't care less.

"Uh huh" is all I can manage.

Kyle opens a cupboard under the sink and pulls out a washcloth, which he moistens with tap water. "You got a little in your hair," he says, wiping it away. "You must have caught some bug. Some of my buddies were sick this week, too. One minute they're fine, and the next thing you know, they're heaving. Of course, it might have been because they were out partying too much the night before." He grins.

I wonder how Monica could possibly not like Kyle.

Then Julie comes in and says something about a 24-hour virus going around, and wants to know if she should call my mom. I tell her, "No, don't bother. I feel better. Really." And this is how Monica finds us when she finally gets back from the store—me on the floor, Kyle beside me, and Julie leaning against the doorjamb.

"What's going on?" Monica asks. She gives me a long look.

"Hey, Sis," Kyle says in mock sweetness. "Nice get-up."

Monica is wearing black thigh-high stockings, a red plaid miniskirt, and a red sweater with a denim vest. She ignores him altogether.

"We think Ali has that virus that's going around," Julie says. "Why don't you give her a ride home, Monica? If you feel up to it, that is," she says, looking at me.

"Yeah," I say. "I'm ready." All I want to do is get out of there.

We're quiet on the drive to my house. Monica pulls her car into my driveway, puts it in park, then glances over and says, "You still look green. Wow, I didn't know anyone could *actually* turn that color."

"Gee, *thanks*, Mon. You're really helping."

"Sorry. I didn't mean it like that."

"Give me a minute, okay?" I can't go in and face my parents just yet.

"Sure," she says. "I'm in no hurry."

We sit for a while, listening to a new song on the radio. "Kyle doesn't seem that bad," I say, and tell her about how he wiped vomit from my hair.

"Oh, *pleeease*. He was *flirting* with you."

"Right . . . *First* he tells me I look *terrible*. Then he's getting *puke* out of my hair. He was *definitely coming on* to me."

"Have you told Matt yet?" she asks, showing no appreciation for my sarcasm.

I sigh. "No."

"Why not?"

"I don't know . . . I'm not sure I want to involve him."

"Don't you think that's sort of weird?"

"No."

Monica gives me this look. "Ali," she says in a serious voice.

"Yeah?"

"He has a right to know."

Chapter 5

Coffee is the drug of choice in Lakeview. On Saturday mornings, the line at Java House stretches to the front door. Today, Monica works the bar so I don't have to deal with the espresso beans. Lately, the smell of beans makes me want to wretch.

After the morning rush, Niles Sherman comes in with a girl Monica and I have never seen before. She has strawberry blonde hair, and her eyes are rimmed with heavy black eyeliner. All it takes is one look at Monica, and I know she's thinking the same thing: *What happened to Robin Evans?*

"Hey, Lois," he says to me, then looks at Monica and nods.

He orders a double espresso, then slips his hand into the girl's back pocket and whispers in her ear. She laughs and orders a white chocolate mocha with double whip.

You'd never know that Monica and Niles hooked up this summer. You'd never guess he used to throw pebbles at her window, or that they'd make out in his car afterward. Monica's already over Niles. She's moved on to guy number 16, Dylan Lang. He graduated last year and works construction, so he's perpetually tanned and buff. He came in one day last month for coffee and asked her out. They go out from time to time. Tonight, he's taking her to dinner and a movie. Unlike Niles, Dylan is a date-night kind of guy, but I have my doubts about him. He went out with Rena Albright all last year, but told Monica they'd just broken up. When he comes in for coffee, he's always checking out the girls, and he never calls Monica when he says he will. I think he's a dog. Naturally, Monica's crazy about him.

Just before Niles and Eyeliner Girl leave, Monica asks him the one thing that's on both of our minds.

"Where's Robin?"

"Uh . . . I dunno," he says. "Haven't seen her lately."

❦

I stop by Matt's house on the way home from work. His parents are both working today. His mom's a nurse's assistant at Memorial Hospital, and his dad's a carpenter. Both work some weekends, leaving Matt at home to babysit his brother and three sisters. The whole way over, I tell myself that if I can get Matt alone for a while, I'll tell him. Monica's right. He does have a right to know. Besides, I've always been up front with Matt about everything.

When I get there, Matt's in his room burning a CD. "I just finished," he says. "You want to hear it?"

"Sure."

He locks his door, turns the stereo on low, then pulls me down on the bed and kisses me. And though I'm nervous about telling him, I get that rush I always do whenever we're together.

"Matt . . ." I start.

"Shhh," he says, placing a finger over my lips. "It's okay. Daniel's outside with his friends . . . Megan's asleep . . . Sarah and Amy are at the neighbors . . ."

His arms tighten, he presses against me, and the kiss gets hard and deep. I love the way he smells—slightly musky and spicy. He runs his fingers through my hair and kisses me again. At first, we're just listening to the music, and kind of making out. I want to tell him to stop because I have something to tell him. But before I know it, he slips his hand underneath my shirt and he's rolling on top of me. All I can hear is my heartbeat.

"You feel so good," he says, kissing me everywhere. "I love to feel you next to me."

"Matt . . . No . . . Not with Megan down the hall," I say, pulling my shirt down.

"Okay . . . okay." He groans, then smiles. "You're right . . . I'll be good . . . Promise."

I curl up next to him and trace his profile with my finger.

You'd think I would tell him right there and then, but I don't. All I want is to be here with Matt and to forget, just for a little longer. We lay there, holding each other, for a while, and then Matt falls asleep. I love to watch him sleep. He's really beautiful, which is a strange thing to say about a guy, but he is. I think about waking him, so we can talk, but I don't. I wish I could freeze time and keep the world on the other side of the door. Maybe Monica's right. Maybe I am in denial. But it doesn't matter. I figure there'll be plenty of time to tell him later.

I don't want Matt's parents to come home early and find me in his room, so I get up. I check on Megan, who's still sleeping, and Daniel, who's still playing outside with his friends. Then Sarah and Amy come back from the neighbors, so I watch a video with them in the family room.

Matt's mom still isn't home at 3:30. "She must have forgotten I'm working tonight," Matt says, checking his watch. He's already dressed for work in his Vincent's Market polo shirt and black pants.

"I can stay until she gets back," I say. I'm helping the girls put on make-up that Amy had gotten for her birthday last week.

"Great . . . thanks," Matt says. He leans down and kisses me. He tastes minty, like toothpaste. "I'll stop by your house after work. Okay?"

"Sure," I say, thinking I'll tell him tonight. By the time Matt comes over, my parents will probably be in bed.

When I finish doing their make-up, the girls *really, really, really* want to do mine. They come at me, giggling and laughing, holding red lipstick and blue eye shadow, and Amy almost pokes me in the eye with the applicator for the eye shadow. Then Megan comes out of her room with her blanket, plops in my lap, and starts sucking her thumb. By the time Mrs. Ryan comes home, I look like some hoochy girl.

"Hi, Ali," she says, looking surprised to see me there. Obviously, Matt didn't mention I was coming over today. She's carrying a bag of groceries.

"Hi, Mrs. Ryan."

When she sees my face, she laughs. "Let me guess," she says. "Sarah and Amy?"

I nod.

"Where's Matt?"

"He had to be at work by 4:00, so I offered to stay until you got back."

"I'm sorry," she says. "I thought he had to be there at 4:30."

"It's okay. I didn't have any plans."

"Well, thanks. I appreciate it."

Mrs. Ryan was really nice when we first met, but since the summer, she's been different—cooler. I mentioned it to Matt, and he admitted that his mom thought we were getting too serious. The worst part is Matt told his mom we were sleeping together— Mrs. Ryan had asked. She wanted to make sure we were being responsible. Mrs. Ryan has never said anything to me about it, but it's embarrassing that she knows.

"Well, I better go . . ."

"Matt tells me you're applying to Northwestern," Mrs. Ryan says.

"Uh, yeah." I don't say anything about our new plan. I'm not sure whether Matt told her.

"That's wonderful, Ali. I've heard they have an excellent journalism program," she says while putting away cans of soup. "I ran into Matt's guidance counselor last week, and he tells me that Matt will probably qualify for the scholarship at Pratt. His father and I are both thrilled. You know, Matt will be the first Ryan to go to college."

"Oh . . . I didn't know that," I say. It had never occurred to me.

Mrs. Ryan keeps chattering. "I know it'll be hard on you and Matt next year, going to schools so far away from each other, but it'll be good for you both to meet other people." She doesn't look at me—she keeps her eyes on the grocery bag she's folding. I can tell when I'm being managed, but I don't know what to say. All I can think is, *thank God,* they'll never know. His parents would freak out if they knew, and they'd probably hate me, too. No, they'd *definitely* hate me.

⚜

The rest of the day, I think about what Monica said—how Matt has a right to know. But when Matt comes by after work, my parents are still up watching a movie in the family room. He tells me he'll be working a double shift tomorrow. I'll just wait. It doesn't matter. It's not as if one more day is going to make a difference.

We sit on the sofa in the den and listen to music and talk. He's in such a good mood. He gives me a pomegranate from Vincent's. The other day, when he was telling me he had to draw pomegranates in class, I said I'd never eaten one. He always remembers things like that. Later, when we're in the kitchen, he shows me how to cut it. He also tells me about a fishing trip he's going on soon with his dad and brother. They're planning to camp near some lake in Wisconsin his dad heard about and fish for musky. It's the same weekend I have my appointment at Planned Parenthood, but I can't tell him that.

Then my dad comes in and tries the pomegranate, too. They start talking about musky and the best type of bait to use, but I'm not really listening. All I think is that I've got to tell Matt soon, and what a relief it'll be when he finally knows.

Chapter 6

On Monday morning, I wake up feeling worse than usual. I throw up twice while getting ready for school, and, believe it or not, that helps. I almost feel normal afterward, but when Monica gives me a ride to school, my nausea starts all over again. Monica's dad bought her a little red sports car for her sixteenth birthday. She calls it the "Bribemobile" because he gave it to her the same day he introduced her to his new girlfriend, who is only seven years older than Monica. When you ride in it, you feel every bump in the road, and today it's making me sick.

As soon as I walk into school, I know I'm going to vomit. There's no time to race to the bathroom. I bolt toward a waste can near the lockers, where I puke this morning's breakfast. Fortunately, no one is around.

"That's revolting," says Monica. "What did you eat this morning?" She's rummaging around in her backpack for what I hope will be a tissue.

"Cereal . . . with raspberries," I say, wiping my mouth with the tissue Monica finally produces.

"Avoid that next time."

"What are you? The food police?" I'm trying to be funny, but it's a real effort this morning, considering how I feel. "It looked good at the time."

Monica laughs, but then gets serious. "So, are you going to tell Matt?"

"After school," I say. "He's giving me a ride home."

✑

By second period study hall, I'm not feeling any better, and I'm debating whether I should go home now. Matt's sitting at the desk across the aisle from me, but he doesn't notice anything. I try to convince myself I'm just fine—mind over matter and all that. But it doesn't work. Finally, I stand up, thinking I'll tell Mrs. Fortner I need to go home. But it's too late—it comes over me all at once like a wave. I feel dizzy and hot, and suddenly I throw up right there on the floor. Not a lot, but enough to make quite a scene. Mrs. Fortner gives me a long look. Everyone stares. I wish the floor would open and swallow me up. It doesn't, so I say something idiotic and dash out of the room.

When the bell rings, signaling the end of second period, I'm sitting on a bench outside study hall. Matt's the first one out the door. He's carrying a notebook I left behind.

"Hey, are you okay?" He looks really concerned.

"Yeah."

He sits down next to me and rubs my back. "I wanted to come after you, but Fortner wouldn't let me."

"She came looking for me in the bathroom," I say.

"What do you have?" he asks. "The flu or something?"

"I'm pregnant," I say. And just like that, it's out.

He turns white. Students pass by, talking and laughing. I hear a locker slam somewhere down the hall. Some of the kids stare as they walk by, maybe guessing that some personal drama is playing out.

"Are you serious?" His voice is a whisper.

"Yes." I start to cry.

He shakes his head. "I thought you got your period."

"I thought so, too . . . but it wasn't a regular period."

He shakes his head. "I don't get it. How did *this* happen?"

How?! How could he forget the one time we hadn't used any protection? Sure, I'd put it out of my mind, but I never really forgot about it. I give him a look, and I can see in his eyes that he knows exactly what I'm thinking about—the time we hadn't used anything. It wasn't like us to do something so stupid. We had totally convinced ourselves it was okay. It wouldn't happen to us, but we were wrong.

Matt stands up, as if he's going to leave, then turns, swears, and kicks the bench hard. Neither of us says anything for a while. He doesn't look at me. When the bell rings again, all he says is, "I've got to go." Then he walks away.

I stay for a few more minutes, thinking he'll turn back any second and tell me everything will be okay, that we'll work it out together. I'd thought it would be such a relief to finally tell him, but it isn't—not at all.

⸎

As it turns out, I get my stomach under control after study hall, so I decide to stay for the rest of my classes. After school, I'm in the parking lot with Monica when Matt drives up.

"Hey . . . I'll give you a ride home," he says. "We need to talk." People stream by, heading to their cars and calling out to their friends. Some guy in a truck lays on the horn.

Monica won't even look at Matt. When I told her how he reacted, she was totally disgusted. Matt doesn't say a word when I get in, but he reaches for my hand and laces his fingers around mine. Taking some back roads lined with trees, we drive to the place we always go to when we want to be alone—a country road that ends near a field. Today, a few horses are off in the distance.

Finally, he says, "Look, I'm sorry."

"It's okay." I know it took him by surprise, and besides, it's not like I handled it so well myself either. It took me forever to tell him.

"It's just that . . . I didn't think this could possibly happen to us."

"I know . . . Me, too."

He's quiet for a long moment. "How long have you known?"

"About a week . . . officially."

"A *week!* Why didn't you say something earlier?"

"I could never seem to find the right time to tell you . . . and I was still hoping it wasn't true."

He nods miserably and pulls me close. "You should have told me sooner." He holds me so tightly I can feel his heart pounding. We sit like that for a while. I start to cry, and I just can't stop. Finally, he lets go, rummages around in the glove compartment, and hands me a napkin.

"So?" he says, looking at me. I see all the questions there in his eyes.

"So . . . I've already made an appointment to have an . . ." I can't even say the word, and fortunately, I don't have to.

Matt gets it right away. He nods, looking relieved. "It's the only way," he says. "It'll be all right."

"Matt," I say, starting to cry again.

"It's okay. We'll get through this together, okay? I love you."

My parents have no idea what's going on. My mother is happy I'm eating meat again. I know she thinks being a vegetarian was just some phase I was going through. If she knew the real reason I'm back to my carnivorous ways, she'd spaz. She makes meat every night this week—roast beef, grilled pork chops, spaghetti and meatballs. I eat it all. And though I'm throwing up every day, I gain three pounds.

The rest of the week seems endless. All I can think about is my appointment at Planned Parenthood. And it's all Matt and I talk about now. He wants to go with me, but he and his dad have been planning this fishing trip for months. We think up all kinds of excuses for him not to go, but all of them fall flat.

On Wednesday, I finally say, "Just go on your trip. It's okay . . . Monica said she'd go with me." Both of us already asked for the day off. Matt's upset that he won't be there, and I'm not exactly happy about it, but what other choice do we have?

The rest of the week, I count down the days . . . two more, one more . . . Friday night, I go to bed early, and all I can think is that by this time tomorrow, it will all be over.

Chapter 7

It's Saturday, November seventh, the day I've been waiting for. Without even thinking, I pull on a t-shirt, sweater, and jeans. Then I take one look at myself in the full-length mirror and notice I'm wearing all black. I'm the perfect mourner on the way to a funeral. I think about wearing something a little brighter, but that seems obscene. When Monica picks me up, she stares but doesn't say a word. It's one of those cool, cloudy days. We take the train into Chicago, and this time it takes a little longer than last time to find a cab.

It's freezing outside.

My head hurts.

I think I'm going to puke.

We're silent all the way there. Neither of us feels like talking. When the cab pulls up to 1200 North LaSalle, my stomach shifts into overdrive and starts churning. Monica pays the cab driver, and as soon as I climb out of the cab, a guy not much older than me, in a navy polo shirt and a sweater that makes him look preppy, hands me a flyer. I glance at the flyer from Prep Boy. There are only three words on the flyer: "Stop the Killing!" Underneath is a picture of a fetus that is six weeks old. Then this older, grandmotherly woman wearing a gold cross on a chain starts right in as if we're in the middle of a conversation. "Honey," she says, touching my arm, as if we know each other. "It's not a choice; it's a child. Don't do it. You'll regret it the rest of the your life." I open my mouth, but nothing comes out. Then she says, "Wait. Let me get you some information."

I'm not sure what to do, so I freeze. Then an older man, wearing a blue vest that says "Pro-Choice," walks up to me and says, "Let me help you." He escorts me to the front door. Prep Boy immediately gives up on me and moves toward Monica, thrusting a flyer her way. Monica takes the flyer, rips it in half, and tosses it on the ground. Prep Boy charges after her with another flyer in hand. Then another escort appears and helps Monica.

Monica groans when Prep Boy follows behind her. She turns around and glares at him like a lunatic. I've never seen Monica like this before. "Back off or I'm going to scream," she yells. "You're stalking me!" Prep Boy glances at me, then Monica, shrugs, and walks away. Monica has excellent communication skills.

I glance back at the group of people hanging out next to the curb. I didn't notice them when the cab pulled up, but there are four of them—three women and Prep Boy. They don't look anything like the protestors I've read about in the newspaper—the ones accused of bombing clinics and shooting doctors and patients. One woman with long dark hair drops to her knees and starts praying. The older woman looks right at me with sad, watery eyes, and starts saying the rosary. Another woman who reminds me a little of my mother is carrying a sign that reads: "Wasn't *Your* Mother Pro-Life?"

For some crazy reason, I want to go back and explain to them why I'm here. I want to make them understand. I mean, it's not as if anyone wants to have an abortion—right? Sometimes, though, it's the only way. But by then, we're at the front door. My escort opens the door for Monica and me. As we're walking through the door, I glance down at the flyer again. Monica looks at me. "Are you okay?" she asks. I nod. Then Monica takes the flyer, crumples it, and tosses it in the garbage.

Once we're inside, Monica and I both check in at the security booth. A counselor I'd talked with on the phone explained this was necessary for our own safety. An older woman there asks me for identification and then checks for my name on a sheet of paper. I explain that Monica is my friend, and the woman asks her to show identification, too.

When we get to the reception area, there are already about thirteen other people waiting. I wonder if they're all here for abortions. Monica takes a seat while I check in. Ancient Wise Woman is not here today. I wish she were. A different receptionist takes my name and hands me a clipboard with some forms to fill out. When I woke up this morning, I felt nervous, but now that I'm here, I feel even worse. My hands start shaking, and they just won't stop.

I take a seat next to Monica and look around, but no one looks my way. Everyone is thumbing through magazines or filling out forms. I look down at my forms. My hand is so sweaty that the pen slips out and falls to the floor. I find it underneath my chair. First, I fill out the consent form for the abortion, then a financial consent form. The self-assessment form is much harder to complete. There's a list of questions that need to be answered. The first one is "On a scale of 1 to 10, how confident do you feel about your decision today?" I want to circle five, but I know that won't exactly sail with the counselor. I drop the pen again, pick it up, check the clock on the wall, and circle number eight, which I feel says *confident-but-seriously-freaking-out-to-be-here*. Then I think of college and Matt and my parents, put a big X through the eight, and circle ten instead.

There are other questions to answer. "Does an abortion conflict with your spiritual beliefs?" *No, but I still can't believe I'm here.* "Will this affect your relationship with your partner or family?" *Matt: No. Parents: Oh my God, I don't even want to think about it.* "Do you have a support system for your decision?" *Sure.*

Plus, there's a list of common emotions, and the form asks you to circle the ones that describe how you're feeling. I circle "nervous," "anxious," "afraid," "relieved," "conflicted," and "guilty."

When I'm finished, I check the clock on the wall again and return the forms to the receptionist, who asks me to take a seat and wait until my name is called.

I hate being here. I feel sick to my stomach, but it's just nerves—I think.

"You okay?" Monica asks.

"I just want to get it over with."

Monica squeezes my hand, which is clammy because I'm so anxious. A few minutes later, the door opens, and a nurse calls my name. I nearly jump out of my seat.

First, I have an ultrasound. Nora, the health care assistant, explains that this is a vaginal ultrasound and will show how far along I am in my pregnancy. Then I go to the lab, where they check my weight and blood pressure and prick my finger to check my iron level and something else I didn't quite catch.

I ask Nora what time it is. I've only been here an hour and ten minutes, but it feels like forever. Nora leaves, but promises to come right back. I wish they would speed this up. I want to get it over with. My mind is wandering all over the place. There's this videotape playing in my mind. I see the protesters, the flyer, and the picture of the baby my mother showed me that day in the kitchen. I try to turn off the tape, but it's as if someone has glued down the play button. The images won't go away.

For the past two weeks, I've been telling myself I'm having a minor medical procedure on Saturday—like having a cavity filled. But all of a sudden, I'm wondering whether I'm doing the right thing. This is the most important decision I've ever made in my life, and I barely considered my choices. I never even *opened* the packet of information the counselor gave me on my first visit. But when I think about next year and Matt, I remind myself there's no other way.

Nora comes back and asks me to follow her to the counselor's office. Debby is there. Today, she's wearing wire-rimmed glasses. It feels good to see a familiar face. "Ali," she says, as if she's been waiting for me. "Please have a seat."

A file is already on Debby's desk with my name on it, but Debby doesn't open it right away. Instead, she looks at me and says, "How are you feeling about your decision today?"

"Fine."

Debby looks at me for a second. She doesn't look completely convinced.

"Shall we review the other options again?"

"Uh, no." I shake my head vigorously to prove that I'm fine, that there's no need to go over all that again. I feel tense, and my hands are shaking again. I grip onto the seat so Debby won't notice, and I turn my attention to the window behind her desk. The clouds are just starting to break, and sunlight is streaming through the window like a strobe light.

Debby opens my file. "Ali, I was reading over the form you filled out," she says. "The emotions you're feeling—nervousness, fear, anxiety, relief—are all normal for someone about to have an abortion. But I'm concerned about your feelings of conflict and guilt. Why are you feeling these emotions?"

I study my shoes. What does she mean *why*? Doesn't everyone feel somewhat guilty and conflicted? Is anyone absolutely, positively sure? I'm here to terminate my pregnancy because it doesn't fit into my plans.

"I don't know . . ."

"Are you having second thoughts?"

"Not really," I say, thinking about Matt and college. But then I say, "I do want children someday, but this isn't the right time. I guess I feel sort of guilty about the timing."

The counselor nods and studies me. I hold my breath. "That's understandable," she says, flipping through my chart. "Ali," she finally says, "you're eleven weeks pregnant. You have time to think about this some more. If you'd like, you could take a few days or even another week. Maybe you should talk it over again with someone you trust."

I shake my head. *"No,* I need to take care of this today. I've already spent a lot of time thinking about my options," I say. *(Liar, liar, pants on fire.)*

Debby nods, but doesn't look persuaded. "All right then," she says, looking at me for a long moment.

Debby explains what will happen next. I listen closely at first, but then I tune in and out. "The doctor will insert a speculum . . . next your cervix will be dilated . . . you'll feel strong cramping . . . take slow deep breaths . . . you'll feel a gentle suction of an aspirator . . . someone will be there to assist you."

Finally, Debby asks, "Do you have any questions?"

"How long is this going to take?"

"Five to seven minutes."

"Other questions?"

"No," I say and shake my head. *I just want to get this over with.*

Debby leads me down a hallway that smells vile, so I try not to breathe in. (It doesn't work.) Then she opens the door to a small room. She instructs me to undress from the waist down and reminds me that we'll meet again after the procedure.

I sit on the exam table with a white paper sheet wrapped around my waist. The room is cool, and I'm starting to shake, but I know this has nothing to do with the temperature. I tuck my legs under me and try not to think about why I'm here and what's going to happen. There's a machine in the corner that's covered with a cloth, but I know that is the vacuum. It's not nearly as scary-looking as I thought it would be, but I decide not to look at it anyway. I will make myself go numb. I will not think about why I'm here. It will all be over in a few minutes, and then I can get out of here.

I check the clock a dozen times and start pacing the room. I stop to look at a print on the wall—a Diego Rivera—one of my mom's favorite artists. The picture is of a woman with dark skin and dark hair, wearing a bright purple dress and staring right at me. She's plump and round and seems to be saying, "Are you sure you know what you're doing?" Then I realize I'm standing next to the vacuum and jump back.

The smell is still getting to me. *How can these people work here with that smell?!* My stomach rumbles, and my throat goes dry. I sit back down and stare at the print. I can't stop looking at it. I ate a bagel this morning because the counselor told me I should eat something, but it's not helping at all. I feel hot all of a sudden and try to sit very still, but it hits me fast, and there's no holding back. I swing my legs off the table and sprint to the waste can.

When the doctor and her assistant walk in, there I am, on the floor, kneeling over the waste can and holding the paper sheet around my waist with one hand. There's vomit in my hair, but I don't care. All I can think about is this tiny little person growing inside me. My mind keeps flashing that baby picture my mom showed me, with the sweet innocent face and perfect mouth. And for the first time, I wonder what my baby will look like. I wonder whether it's a boy or a girl. That's when I know I can't go through with it.

⌘

"And then you bolted?" Monica says.

"Yep." I grin and take a bite of my burger—double cheese, extra pickle, hold the onion. I can't get enough of them these days. We're at a fast-food place we found around the corner from Planned Parenthood.

We're sitting by a window, the sun is out, and it feels like a completely different day. For the first time in weeks, I feel pretty good, which is weird considering that my life has just taken a drastic turn, and I have no idea where I'm heading.

"Then I ran into Debby. She showed me these fetal develop-ment pictures. Right now, the baby's heart has already begun to beat, and the arms and legs are beginning to form."

"That's amazing," says Monica, "considering it exists mostly on hamburgers and French fries." She takes a sip of her milkshake. "How can you eat like that after you barf?"

"I don't know. It's totally different from having the flu, at least for me. After I get sick, I feel so much better." I take another bite of my hamburger just to prove it.

"Gross."

After lunch and our train ride back to Lakeview, Monica parks her car in the driveway at my house. We just sit there for a while, talking and listening to music. Before I get out, Monica asks, "So what are you going to do?"

"I don't know," I say. "But I'm having this baby."

"Are you going to tell your parents now?"

I shrug. The truth is, I know I have to. All of a sudden, the reality of what I've done hits me, and I'm beginning to wonder if walking out of Planned Parenthood was such a bright idea. Things will never be the same again. I feel this as deeply as I've ever felt anything in my life.

Chapter 8

Later that afternoon, I find my mother in her room packing a suitcase. Her bed is covered with neat stacks of clothes. Four pairs of shoes are lined up in a row. Her toiletries are packed in plastic bags. She has a list in her hand, which she keeps checking. She's anal, if nothing else. "Where are you going?" I ask.

She looks at me in astonishment. "Honey, what do you mean, where am I going? Seattle! We've been talking about this trip for weeks!"

"Oh, yeah. I guess I just forgot it was this week." I vaguely recall them talking about it. Dad has a business meeting in Seattle, and Mom is going along to see an old college friend of hers who lives there.

I feel like the universe is smiling down at me. Suddenly, I have another whole week to float along and hope everything will work out. I figure there's no point saying anything now—I'll wait until they get back.

"Well, it kind of crept up on me, too," my mom says. "I've been so busy with that brochure for the birth center."

She looks at me as if she knows where I've been all morning and what's going on in my life. Then she says, "Listen, Ali . . . Aunt Laura's coming to stay with you. I know you'll be on your own at school next year, but I'll feel better knowing you're not here alone this coming week."

I relax. "It's okay." She smiles, clearly relieved, because this is the sort of thing we usually argue about. Then she goes to the closet, pulls out a black sweater dress, and folds it into a neat square.

"Mom, how old were you when you were pregnant?"

She places the dress in the suitcase and is quiet for a few long moments, smoothing out imaginary wrinkles in the dress. "Thirty. Why do you ask?"

"I was just thinking about Aunt Laura. You know, she was talking about her biological clock the other night."

"Oh, that's right. Well, she still has time. Plenty of women wait until their late thirties, early forties, though I can't say I'd want to do it all over again myself. Diapers . . . 2 a.m. feedings . . . I don't have the energy or patience any more."

"What's it like?"

Mom smiles. "It's the most amazing experience. I'll never forget it. And you . . . you were gorgeous . . . big and fat and pink."

"Did it hurt?"

"A little," she says. "But it was worth it. They put you in my arms, and there you were. Just watching you breathe was amazing."

Matt calls later that afternoon from Wisconsin, just as he promised. I'm not exactly sure what to say, but as soon as I hear his voice, I know I can't tell him that I didn't go through with it—not over the phone, anyway.

"Hi," he says.

"Hi."

"Look, I can't talk long, but I've been thinking of you all day. Are you okay?"

"Yeah," I say, which is, *technically*, true.

"Good." He sounds so relieved that I start to feel guilty. "I want to see you as soon as I get back, but we're not pulling in until late tomorrow night. Is it okay if I pick you up on Monday for school?"

"Sure."

"Ali. . . ?"

"Yeah?"

"I love you."

⁂

I had planned to stay home tonight because of everything that happened today. But then Monica shows up at 7:30 and insists we go out. She was supposed to go out with Dylan, but he cancelled at the last minute. She's wearing a fuzzy pink-silver sweater with a black micromini skirt and boots. Her hair is down, curling around her shoulders, and in her pink champagne lipstick and chandelier earrings, she looks amazing.

We usually take Monica's car because the only other option is to drive Mom's white station wagon, which is about as cool as driving an ambulance or a hearse. But tonight Monica begs me to borrow my mom's car so, incognito, we can drive by Dylan's apartment, where she insists we go first. We drive by slowly, so she can get a good look, but his apartment is completely dark.

After that, we stop by Betty's Pizza because I'm suddenly starving. Then we crank up the stereo and make our standard loop, cruising downtown, out past the high school and Burger Heaven, where everyone hangs out in the parking lot. There's nothing going on tonight, so we keep making our loop, which tonight also includes Dylan's apartment on Glenview Avenue. This is the fifth time we've driven past, and as her best friend, I go along with her crazy drive-by plan, but the truth is I'm getting bored and beginning to wonder if she's slightly obsessive compulsive. They make drugs for people like her.

"Tell me *again* why we're doing this?" I ask.

"*I told you* . . . He said he was sick," she says.

"Maybe he's sleeping."

KAREN HART

"But he didn't *sound* sick."

"You don't necessarily have to *sound* sick to *be* sick," I point out.

We turn left on Glenview, and there it is—his ground floor apartment, dark, *again*, same as the last four times.

"*OhmyGod!*" she shrieks, causing me to drop my Betty's lemonade.

I slam on the brakes. "*What!?*" I don't see anything.

"Right there, by the shrubs," she says, pointing to two shadowy figures walking on the sidewalk towards the apartment building's front entrance.

"That's him with . . . Rena Albright."

"Keep driving," she commands, slouching down in her seat, "but go slow."

"I thought they broke up."

"That's what he told me. I knew it. God, I'm such an idiot . . . and I was starting to really like him, Ali. I was."

She sulks the rest of the night. We stop by Vincent's Market, where she buys three candy bars, and proceeds to eat one right after the other. By the time I drop Monica off at home, she's already over him. Dylan Lang, number 16, is history.

꿍

When I wake up Sunday morning, my parents have already left for their trip. I feel sick again, so I try a small bowl of corn flakes, which I regurgitate back into the sink about 15 seconds later. I'd decided to give up eating breakfast entirely, when my aunt arrives with her suitcase and a bag of bagels, still warm from the bakery.

"I just picked these up," she says, opening the bag. "Try one . . . they're amazing."

I pick at a blueberry bagel, and find that not only is it good, but I'm able to keep it down. I eat two. I may have to give up

63

cereal.

Later that afternoon, Aunt Laura and I go to the mall. I can't help but notice all the babies. They're everywhere. When we walk by a baby store, Aunt Laura stops to look at the window display. Draped over a white rocking horse is a blue and white baby blanket. A tiny christening outfit is suspended from the ceiling. All of a sudden, I feel dizzy and weak.

"It's times like this that my biological clock seems to tick loudest," Aunt Laura says. She places an arm around my shoulders and gives me a light squeeze. "A friend of mine at work is pregnant. She's the same age as me, so I've been thinking about it more . . . Hey, are you okay? You look pale."

"I need to sit down a minute."

We find a bench nearby. "Put your head between your knees," she advises.

I try it and feel ridiculous, but it works. Within a few minutes, I start to feel better. "I think I need something to eat."

"Sure," Aunt Laura says. "I know just the place." But I don't miss the look on her face.

Aunt Laura leaves early the next morning so she can catch the 6:30 train back to Chicago from Lakeview. She's already gone when I wake up. It's a good thing, too, because I'm feeling really, really crappy. I take a shower, and everything there makes me sick—the smell of the soap, the shampoo, and even the cream rinse. I can't believe this is normal. Afterwards, I have to lie down for a while. When I feel better, I put on a pair of jeans and a t-shirt and pull my hair back in a ponytail. I don't bother with any make-up. One whiff of anything unnatural is going to send me straight back into Barfville.

I'm in the kitchen eating a bagel when the doorbell rings. As soon as I open the door, Matt wraps his arms around me and holds me so tightly I can feel his heart beating. "I'm so sorry you had to go through this alone. We'll be more careful . . ."

I pull away. "Matt, we have to talk."

"Sure," he says.

"I didn't do it."

"You didn't . . ."

I shake my head, and when the realization hits him, he gets this awful look on his face.

"I tried, but I couldn't . . ."

"Look, Ali, *you've got to*." He's trying to stay calm, but I can hear the panic in his voice. "We'll make another appointment. I'll go with you this time."

"Matt . . . it won't make any difference. I can't. This is our *baby*." I place a hand on my stomach.

"*So, you're the one making all the decisions?*" The understanding look I'd seen in his eyes just moments ago is now replaced with anger. "I have no input in this at all?"

"What does that mean?"

"It means we should talk about what we should do."

"Which means *what?* That I should have an abortion?"

His voice is tight. "What choice do we have?"

"Matt, this is our baby we're talking about. At first, I told myself it was just a bunch of cells, like a biology project or something. But this is real . . . it's about three inches long . . . the arms and legs are fully formed."

Matt's face gets red, and a muscle near his jaw is twitching. "Ali, I know how you feel, but—"

"Don't tell me you know how I feel, Matt. It's in *my* body, and *you* don't know what it feels like. I've been sick almost every day. If we go for an abortion, *I'm* the one who goes through it. *I'm* the one who has to live with this decision the rest of my life. Don't you get that? I'm having the baby."

"And then what?"

"I don't know. I just can't have an abortion." I reach for him, but he pushes me aside.

"I can tell you one thing I know for sure, Ali. *I don't want a baby.*" He looks at me as if he hates me, then turns around and walks out the door.

I stand there at the doorway and watch him drive away. Then I call Aunt Laura at work and tell her I won't be going to school today. Suddenly, I feel sick—really sick—and the feeling is coming from deep inside.

✺

Matt doesn't call that night, which isn't like him at all. The next day, he's not in study hall. I look for him during lunch, but he's nowhere to be found.

That night, I'm really down. It's an effort to smile, so I can't even pretend everything is okay. Aunt Laura picks up on it right away. When she comes home that night, she walks in with a bag of carry-out. Aunt Laura is not much of a cook. She takes one look at me and asks, "What's wrong?"

"Oh, nothing."

"Did something happen at school?"

"No, nothing like that. Matt and I got into a fight."

"You want to talk about it?"

"Not really."

"Well," she says, "it's normal to have disagreements. After you both cool off, I'm sure you'll work it out."

I feel a little better after that. We eat dinner in the kitchen—egg rolls, an eggplant dish, and spicy chicken. I think about calling Matt, but I don't. Then we watch TV, and I fall asleep on the sofa. I've never done that before, but I feel tired all the time lately.

The next morning before study hall, Matt is waiting for me in the hallway.

"Look," he says, "the other day really took me by surprise.

We need to talk. We have to *do something*, Ali."

He doesn't apologize or anything, but at least we're talking. "I know."

"I have to be at work right after school, but I'll call you later tonight."

"Okay."

After study hall, he walks with me to my next class. At lunchtime, he looks for me in the cafeteria. Things aren't completely normal between us, but I think we're going to be okay. We'll get through this somehow.

I stay after school to edit copy for the November issue of *The Voice*. We always work a month ahead. Andy's there, too. We talk and joke around for a while, but then we both get down to work.

I'm starting to feel sick again, and remember that I haven't eaten since lunch. Yesterday, I called Planned Parenthood and talked to a nurse, who suggested that I carry crackers with me at all times.

I eat a stack of saltines, but they don't help at all, so I start stuffing everything in my backpack.

"You heading out?" Andy says.

"Yeah." I pull on my jacket.

"Need a ride?"

"No, thanks. I drove today."

Andy looks at me closely. "You okay? I mean, you look terrible."

"Gee, thanks, Andy." The truth is I feel terrible, and I know I look terrible. Aren't you supposed to glow when you're pregnant? I crumple a piece of paper and throw it at him, aiming for his head. Andy, laughing at the effort, ducks.

When I get home, I still feel sick. Aunt Laura isn't there yet, so I lie down in my room for a while. When I wake up, it's already dark outside, and Aunt Laura is sitting on the edge of the bed.

"Oh, you're home," I say.

"I just got in." Aunt Laura has an odd expression on her face. "Ali, is there any special reason you're so tired lately?"

"I don't know. Maybe I'm coming down with something."

Aunt Laura doesn't say anything. She brushes a strand of hair off my forehead. "If there's something on your mind, we can talk," she says.

"Thanks, but everything's fine."

"Okay," she says, getting up. "I brought home a pizza. Why don't you come downstairs and have a bite—if you feel up to it, that is."

"Sure. I'll be right there." Actually, I don't feel like eating anything, but I want to prove to Aunt Laura I'm just fine.

But when I walk into the kitchen, the smell of pizza hits me all at once. I run back up the stairs, barely making it to the bathroom in time. Afterwards, I sit there on the floor, next to the bathtub, feeling weak and shaky.

Aunt Laura stands there for a minute, a knowing look on her face, then gets a washcloth from the cabinet and dampens it before handing it to me. I drape it over my face. I want to tell Aunt Laura that it's nothing but some weird flu bug, but I have a feeling she already knows the truth.

I pull the washcloth off. "I'm pregnant."

"I thought so." She's much calmer about it than my mother would be.

"Are you going to tell Mom and Dad?" I ask.

"No, honey, I won't. You should do that. Does this have anything to do with why you and Matt had a fight?"

That's when I tell her everything. Aunt Laura just sits there and listens, as if hearing that your seventeen-year-old niece is pregnant is the most natural thing in the world. Finally, Aunt Laura says, "What are you going to do?"

"I'm going to have the baby." It sounds strange saying it aloud like that.

"Are you planning to keep it?"

"I don't know."

Aunt Laura nods. "You need to tell your mom and dad right away, Ali."

"Mom and Dad are going to freak."

"Give them some credit," she says. "I think they'll handle it better than you think."

Later that night, Matt calls. I didn't think the day could possibly get any worse, but Matt tells me his grandfather died today. Matt's really upset—I can tell by his voice.

"What happened?"

"Another heart attack, but this time he didn't make it."

He tells me they're leaving tonight for Wisconsin to be with his grandmother, and he won't be back until after the funeral sometime next week.

"Matt, I'm sorry."

"Thanks."

After I hang up, I can't help but think how this couldn't have happened at a worse time. Then I feel awful because I know I shouldn't feel that way.

The last night before my parents come home, my aunt gives me a book. It's called *So You're Expecting*. . . and it has all this information about being pregnant and what to expect each month. Then we make eggs and toast for dinner because she thinks it will be easier on my stomach than take-out food.

"How am I going to tell them?" I ask while we're cleaning up after dinner.

"There's no easy way," she says. "You'll just have to sit them down and tell them the truth. When are you planning to do it?"

"I think I'll wait until after Matt gets back." Aunt Laura arches an eyebrow.

"When do you think I should tell them?"

"As soon as possible," she says. "Not the minute they walk in the door tomorrow, but sometime over the weekend."

Chapter 9

My parents return home Friday, but by Saturday night, I still haven't told them. That night, Monica picks me up. We were planning to go to a movie, but we decide to skip it at the last minute. Instead, we drive around awhile just talking and then stop for ice cream, even though it's freezing outside. Just *thinking* about telling my parents is making me nervous. Ever since my parents came back, I've been shaking inside.

Finally, Monica says, "God, look at you. You're a wreck! You have to tell them, Ali. I know it's going to be hard, but once you do . . . at least that part will be over."

"My parents are going to freak out."

"No, they won't," says Monica. "Your parents will discuss this with you rationally, and they'll counsel you."

I shoot her a look. Monica has no idea what it's like to be cursed with a functional family. My parents have only one expectation for me: absolute perfection. "My mom will come completely unglued and my dad . . . oh, God . . . I don't even want to think about it."

That night, I can't sleep, so I lay there, staring at the ceiling, and mentally practice my lines. "Mom, Dad, there's something I need to talk to you about . . . It's serious . . . I should have told you sooner." I have no idea how to go about it, and this isn't exactly the sort of topic they routinely write about in teenage girls' magazines.

I try to imagine my parents' reaction, and every scenario I come up with is awful. Last year, a girl from my class, Rachel

Thomas, got pregnant. I didn't know her personally, but I heard that her mother *forced* her to get an abortion. Mom is pro-life, so there's no way that would happen with me.

When I wake up the next morning, it's not even 7:00, but I get up anyway. I take a shower and then sit on the stool, clutching a towel around me because I feel so crappy. I can't remember any more what it was like to feel normal. When I finally feel better, I look for my blue sweater. Dad loves that sweater on me.

My parents are already in the kitchen, reading the newspaper and sipping coffee. I toast a bagel and spread cream cheese on it, as if this is any other Sunday morning.

Dad gets up to refill his coffee mug. "You're up early today."

"Yeah."

Then, sitting across the table from Mom, I decide to tell them after I've eaten. Part of me just wants to hang on to this last moment of normalcy before my parents go ballistic. But Mom looks up from the paper and says, "Ali, you look pale. Are you feeling all right?"

I take a quick breath and pray that they'll understand. This can't wait any longer. "There's something I need to talk with you about . . ."

They both look at me, but don't have a clue what's coming next.

"I'm pregnant." There, I finally said it.

Everything goes quiet. The words hang in the air.

"You're *what?*" Mom looks at me as if she didn't hear right. Dad's face whitens. I know I'll never forget this moment. Their shock . . . the smell of coffee . . . the paper spread out on the table . . . the sound of the clock.

"I'm pregnant," I say, then look away. I force myself to swallow, to breathe.

Dad drops his coffee mug. It breaks into several chunky pieces, splattering coffee everywhere. He ignores the mess and sits down in his chair, running a hand through his hair and making it stand on end. The vein above his left eye is bulging—it always does that whenever he's stressed.

There's a seemingly endless silence, except for the clock ticking on the kitchen wall. *Tick, tock, tick, tock.* I wish I were dead.

Then Mom says, "Are you sure? Have you been to a doctor?" She sounds scary calm, as if we're discussing SAT scores or prom dresses.

"Yes. I had a pregnancy test at a clinic."

More silence. For days now, I imagined how they would react when I told them. I expected Dad to rant, and Mom to cry. What I hadn't expected was this—this is even worse.

"I just don't understand how this could happen, Allison," says my mother, starting to unravel. "You're intelligent—an A student. We've talked about sex at home, and you've had years of sex education at school." Her voice starts to rise, and now she comes completely unglued. *"Dammit, Ali, how could you let yourself get into this situation?"*

I'm not about to give them specifics, so I say, "It was an accident . . . " Then I start crying, but I don't bother to wipe the tears away.

"Do you know how far along you are?" Mom asks.

I hate this, but I know I have to sit here and take it. "About twelve weeks."

"Twelve weeks! Why didn't you tell us before now?"

I shrug.

Mom stands up and starts pacing. "Do Matt's parents know?"

I shake my head, but Mom doesn't seem to care one way or the other. "We'll just have it taken care of," Mom says.

Taken care of? "What does that mean?"

Mom totally loses it, and starts yelling, *"Allison, you know what it means. You can't have a baby. You know that! You are seventeen years old . . . a child! Think about your future. A baby would ruin it."*

That gets to me. "You are *such* a hypocrite! All my life, you've been telling me how morally wrong abortion is. How can you sit there and tell me we'll 'take care of it'?"

Mom lowers her voice. "Ali, be reasonable. It's the only way. There are some situations where there's just no other—"

"I am *not* having an abortion. All right? Believe me, I know. I already tried." My voice breaks, and I start crying all over again.

"You did?" Dad asks.

I nod.

Mom sits down. Both of them still look shocked. "Maybe you should have thought of that before . . ." Mom says tightly.

"Katherine," says Dad.

"*Dammit!*" she says, smacking the kitchen table with her hand. "How can someone so smart be so stupid?" She jumps up and walks out of the room, but she storms right back. I've never seen her like this before.

"Kate . . ." he says again. He's the calmest one in the room. "That's enough. I think we all ought to think about it for a while before we say something we might regret."

Mom is slightly calmer, but she's not about to back off yet. "Neither of you seems to understand the ramifications of having a baby." Her eyes lock on me. "Once you have that baby, whether you keep it or not, it will change your life forever in ways you cannot yet imagine. This baby is nothing more than a speck right now. It is not—"

"Mom . . ."

"Kate," Dad says. "Let's all calm down and talk about what to do later."

Mom sits down, looking defeated, and stares out the window. Dad turns to me and takes my hand in his. "The important thing is you. Are you okay?"

I can't talk.

"Your mom only wants what's best for you, Ali. We both do. We're just . . . stunned." He lets out a long sigh. "Give us some time to let this sink in. Okay?" He rubs his temples.

"Okay."

Finally, Mom says, "I'm going to take you to my gynecologist on Monday. I want you to see someone I trust. Then we can discuss your options."

"Okay." The last thing I need is another pregnancy test, but I'm not about to argue with her. It's easier to be agreeable. "But there's something you should know. I won't have an abortion. It's just not right—not for me. The baby's part of me . . . Doesn't that mean anything to you?"

"More than you possibly can know," Mom says, looking me squarely in the eyes. "You're talking about my grandchild." Then she walks out of the room, leaving me alone with my father. He takes one look at me, then pulls me close and gives me a hug.

⁓

I hide out in my room the rest of the day. The kitchen has become Mission Control. Dad's voice is low and calm; Mom's is shrill and erratic, bouncing off the walls, full of panic. I'm a good little girl and clean my room, but I keep going into the hallway to listen. I can't make out what they're saying.

At 4:30, Monica calls. "What gives?"

I give her the blow-by-blow details. Before we hang up, she tells me about some new guy she met, a college boy who works in the shoe department at Wolf's Department Store. He becomes number 17. She met him this afternoon at the mall, which is classic Monica. Less than 24 hours after finding out that Dylan blew her off for someone else, she's already got some new guy after her.

"What's he like?"

"Cute . . ."

"But?"

"But kind of dull. I mean, he has his whole life mapped out, and he's only nineteen years old."

Later that night, there's a knock on my door. "Come in." I'm sitting on my bed with my homework spread out, pretending to work.

Mom walks in and sits on the edge of the bed next to me. Her eyes are red and her face is blotchy. She's holding a tissue that's now a crushed, wet ball.

"Ali, I want to apologize for this morning. I didn't handle the news very well. It's just that . . . I was so surprised. When I was your age, we didn't talk much about sex with our parents. But things are so different now. You and your friends are much more informed than we ever were. I never thought this could happen to you."

"Neither did I."

"I'm going to call the school in the morning and tell them you won't be there. Then I'll get you in to see my doctor," she says, standing up.

She stops at the doorway, her hand on the knob. "Ali?"

"Yeah?"

"Maybe I should have . . ." But then she stops, shakes her head, and says, "Never mind."

❧

"All I said was that you should think about your options," Mom says. We're sitting in the parking lot at the doctor's office. I just had a pelvic exam, my *third* pregnancy test, and it turns out that, yes, I really *am* pregnant. I feel like I'm stuck in some bad TV sitcom. If my situation weren't so tragic, I'd laugh.

"I do *not* want an abortion. There's no way I could *ever—ever*—do that. And I don't understand you. You've always been so totally against abortion." I can't believe we're still arguing about this.

Mom pulls out of the parking lot. She looks straight ahead,

but tightens her grip on the steering wheel. "Your father and I discussed this at length yesterday." She sighs. "We are not going to make you do anything you don't want. But, Allison, once you have this baby, there's no going back. I want you to promise me you will seriously consider adoption."

"Okay," I say, "but I don't know if I can do that either."

We stop at a red light. Mom turns to me. "I talked with another doctor in the practice while you were having the exam. His name is Dr. Johnson, and he knows of a young couple that can't have children and are interested in adopting a baby. It would be a private adoption. He's a professor at a university, and she's a librarian."

"I don't know." The car behind us toots twice. "The light's green."

"Oh."

We're on Northwest Highway now, heading for home. "How does Dr. Johnson know this couple?"

"They went to college together. Just think about it, Ali. They're in their early thirties, and they could give this baby everything you can't right now—a home, a stable life, a two-parent family." Mom pulls into the garage and turns off the ignition. "Before you decide one way or the other, you could meet them. Dr. Johnson says he can arrange it."

"Let me think about it."

"Of course." She reaches out and tucks a strand of hair behind my ear. She looks like maybe she's starting to understand how I feel.

❧

Matt calls me that night. He and his family just got back from Wisconsin. He's telling me he'll be back in school tomorrow and wants to talk, but I stop him.

"Matt, I told my parents. I went to my mom's gynecologist

today."

"You told your parents?"

"Yes. You should probably tell your parents as soon as possible."

Neither of us says anything for a while. I can tell he's upset. Then, he says, "What did they do?"

"It was awful at first, but it's better now. Mom wants me to give the baby up for adoption. Matt, I—" I want to tell him I'm not sure I can give the baby up, but he cuts me off.

"I can't believe you," he says. "I can't believe you didn't wait until I came back." Then, *click.* He's gone.

Chapter 10

On Tuesday, Niles brings a word to share in English class. "Excellent," says Carrot Top, smiling with approval. "What's your word?"

"Concupiscence," Niles says, sitting straight in his chair for a change, star student of the hour.

Carrot Top tilts her head to one side and says the word aloud. She looks baffled, something we haven't seen so far this year. "CON-CU-PISCENCE," she says very slowly, syllable by syllable. "Let's write it on the chalkboard. How do you spell that exactly?" she asks.

Niles feeds her each letter, and she transcribes it on the blackboard. "Very good, Mr. Sherman," says Carrot Top, nodding her head with approval. "I don't know this word. Will you please share its meaning with us?"

Niles and a group of boys snicker. Monica and I share a look. We both know something is up.

"It means sexual desire, Mrs. Frye," he says, all wide-eyed innocence. "And lust."

Everyone laughs. Someone in the back row starts hooting and stamping his feet. And this guy, Rob Herzog, yells out, *"Did you say sexual desire?!"*

Carrot Top turns an interesting shade of red, then erases every trace of "concupiscence" from the board, her hand shaking the whole time. Outbursts make her nervous. Something tells me Niles won't be getting extra credit for this word.

Second period study hall: No Matt.

Lunchtime: Missing again.

"What's with you two?" Monica asks over a grilled cheese sandwich in the cafeteria.

"He's freaking out."

"He better *un-freak*, so you guys can figure out what to do."

"He just needs time, I guess." I don't know what I expected, but I didn't think he'd avoid me like the plague.

"Eat," Monica commands. When I'm upset, it's a real effort to eat, so Monica has taken it upon herself to see that I act in the baby's interest. I dip a cracker in my tomato soup and take a bite just to please her.

"And don't forget to eat that salad. You need your greens." She's so bossy these days. She's been reading the book Aunt Laura gave me, mostly for moral support, and now considers herself an expert on prenatal care. "You know what I think about Matt?" she asks, opening a bag of chips. "*Too freaking bad!* I mean, *geez*, it's happening to you, too."

"I know."

"How's it going with your parents?"

"My mom's still pushing for adoption. It's all she talks about."

Monica nods. She and I talk about adoption all the time. In fact, I've talked more with her than Matt about it. She can't see getting tied down with a baby. "It's just something I wouldn't want to deal with at this point in my life," she said once. "But," she said, "you love Matt. I think, somehow, that makes the decision harder." And it does. It really does.

❧

When Monica drops me off after school, Matt's car is parked on the street in front of my house. He's standing on the front doorstep with his hands shoved in his pockets. It's cold and drizzling. He moves from one foot to the other, trying to stay warm.

"Hi," he says.

"Hi." I open the front door and let him in. My parents are still at work, so we have the house to ourselves. "Don't you have to work tonight?" I ask.

"I called in sick."

He follows me into the family room. *At least he's here*, I tell myself, but I hope we don't have another bad scene. I sit on the sofa, and he sits on an ottoman across from me.

"Look, I'm sorry I've been such a jerk."

"It's okay." It isn't, but I don't want to get into it.

"So what do you think?" he says.

"You mean about an abortion?"

He nods.

"I'm not having one, Matt. There's just no way I can do it."

"You know, Ali, a lot of people have them. Ryan Slater's girl-friend . . ."

"Meg had an abortion?"

He nods.

"Look, Matt . . . I can't. It *is* a big deal to me."

"Ali . . ." He shakes his head.

All of a sudden, I feel like I'm starting my period. "I'll be right back," I say and leave the room.

When I come back, Matt is still on the ottoman, but now he's resting his head in his hands. "I'm bleeding," I say. I wonder if I'm having a miscarriage. The blood flow is a little heavier than it was the month before I knew I was pregnant.

"You're what?" He looks confused.

"I'm bleeding."

"Are you starting your period?" He sounds relieved and smiles slightly. All I can think is that he doesn't get it at all.

"No, it's not like that . . . but I've got to call the doctor." I find the number for Dr. Bishop, the doctor Mom took me to on Monday. Her office is only fifteen minutes from our house. A nurse answers, and when I explain what's happening, she tells me to come in right away.

Matt doesn't say anything on the way over. As soon as we walk in, a nurse waves us in. When she sees us, she gets this look on her face, and I know what she's thinking. I hate that look. "You can come in, too, if you want," the nurse tells Matt.

We follow the nurse down the hall into an examining room. She's carrying a tray filled with small vials and bandages.

"What's the spotting like?" she asks, wiping the inside of my arm with a wet cotton ball.

"It's pretty light—not like a period."

Matt is looking at a poster that shows the various stages of a fetus growing in a mother's uterus. I watch his face. It's impossible to read him.

"Are you having any cramps?"

"No."

"This will let us know what's going on," says the nurse as she jabs a needle into my arm, filling the vial with blood.

"What kind of a test is it?"

"It's called a Beta-HCG. We'll have the results back tomorrow." The nurse places a clean cotton ball on the spot where she's taken blood and covers it with a bandage. "There's a possibility you could miscarry," she says in a tone that suggests it wouldn't be such a bad thing.

Maybe she's right. A miscarriage would solve everything. Then everything would be back to normal, which would be a huge relief. But somehow the idea of a miscarriage makes me want to cry.

"You should take it easy the rest of the day," the nurse advises. She looks at Matt, then me. "No intercourse, no dancing, no vigorous exercise."

Then she turns to me. "When we get the results back tomorrow morning, we'll call you," she says.

Matt doesn't say a word while he drives me home. When he pulls up in front of my house, he cuts the engine and sits there, staring straight ahead. "Look, I'm sorry. It's just that . . . it didn't seem real to me until today." He reaches for my hand. "It was just this problem that needed fixing, but there . . . in the doctor's office, I realized that 'it' wasn't an 'it.' It's a baby." He's quiet for a while, and then he says, "Whatever you want to do, Ali, is okay with me." Then we hug, and I feel so relieved.

That night, I tell my parents everything. Dad kisses the top of my head, hugs me, and tells me not to worry. Mom doesn't say anything, but she seems slightly relieved, as if maybe this is the answer to her prayers.

The next morning, Mom lets me skip school, and she takes the day off, too. I spend the morning on the sofa surfing the channels. *Click. Click. Click.* If my life were a TV show, I'd be the after-school special or maybe a guest on *Oprah*. My mom works a crossword puzzle at the kitchen table. But every time the phone rings, she jumps up to answer it. Finally, at 11:00, Dr. Bishop's office calls. Mom hands me the phone.

"Everything checked out," the nurse says cheerily. "Looks like you and the baby are doing okay."

⌘

Matt calls later that day from work. "Hey, it's me," he says.
"Hey."
"How were the, uh, test results?" he asks after a pause.
"Fine," I say. "The baby's okay." We don't say anything for a few moments.
Then he says, "I told my parents."
"How'd it go?"
"Uh, not good. My mom was crying when I left. Dad didn't say much of anything, but he slammed his fist in the wall and then poured himself a scotch."
"Was that it?"
"What did you expect?"

"I don't know."

"It was a bad scene."

"I'm sorry."

"It's not your fault."

We're silent for a long time.

"Look," he finally says. "I've got to go."

"Yeah, okay." I want to say something, but don't know what to say any more.

❧

"Wow," is all Monica says at lunch the next day.

"His mom called my mom yesterday," I say.

"What did she say?"

"That Matt and I should take a break from each other. They don't want this to ruin our lives. Blah, blah, blah."

"What's Matt say about all this?"

"Nothing. Just that his mom is hysterical right now . . ." I can't finish. My life is a disaster, and Mrs. Ryan isn't helping things at all.

"Have you and Matt decided what to do?"

"No." Mom is still pushing me to meet the couple Dr. Johnson told her about, but I can't imagine Matt and I handing off our baby to some couple my mother hears about in a doctor's office. I can't imagine this little person growing up and never knowing me—or Matt.

❧

By the end of the month, I've sent in all my college applications—no more forms to fill out, no more writing essays about why I'm so great. I apply to Columbia, NYU, Northwestern, and two backup schools in Illinois. My guidance counselor tells me I should find out by April where I'll be spending the next four years of my life. The thing is, I'd never thought much about what to do after graduation, except for college. But now I have to figure out what to do about the baby, Matt, *and* college. I feel like I have fifteen minutes to map out my entire life.

Chapter 11

What can you say about being seventeen and pregnant except that sometimes it doesn't seem so bad and some days it's overwhelming. On a bad day, I can't stop thinking about it. All I want is for someone to wake me up and tell me it's an awful dream that's moving in incredibly slow motion. On those days, I have to set it aside so I won't drown in it. Monica thinks I'm in denial on those days, but I'm not—not really.

But some days, I have to do that or I would never get out of bed or finish my homework or take a test. I have to remind myself to swallow and breathe and not to think about it too hard or I won't get through the day.

But some days it's easy to forget about it, and it's hard to believe it's actually happening. Maybe because no one knows yet except for a few people: my parents, Matt, his parents, Monica, and Aunt Laura. I'm still not showing, so it's not anything people are talking about. Once in a while, I can actually carry on life as a normal high school senior. Take today, for instance. There's a football game tonight with our arch rival, North View High, which is in the suburb north of Lakeview, so there was a mandatory rally in the gymnasium during sixth period.

Monica and I both hate going to assemblies. We always say we're going to skip out, but for all our pretend rebellion, we never do. So we sit there and eat candy bars that we smuggle in while Monica makes fun of the cheerleaders who never stop bouncing. *"We have spirit, yes we do! We have spirit, how 'bout you?!"* they shout in unison, ponytails flying.

But today, during the rally, I actually caught myself laughing out loud. First, the coaches lined up the football players, blindfolded them, and then told them they were bringing out some hot babes for them to kiss. But instead, out came their mothers. One guy, I swear, looked like he slipped his mother the tongue. Then Brian Swanson, the senior class president, brought out a blender, mixed a Happy Meal in it, and dared someone to drink it. Monica and I didn't think anyone would be stupid enough to do it, but then some freshman with glasses and acne volunteered, and the crowd went nuts.

After the rally, Monica gives me a lift home and stays for a while to hang out. We're in my room listening to music while Monica experiments with eyeliner and I eat nearly an entire bag of cheese puffs—family size. It's scary how much I'm eating.

"You know what I noticed today?" Monica says, looking up for a minute.

"What?"

"Every single cheerleader at our school has blonde hair. I mean it. Every single one. What's up with that?"

I pop another cheese puff into my mouth and shrug. Monica gets this way once in a while. She tried out for the squad freshman year and missed the final cut by one spot. Three years later, she's still not over it.

"Isn't that discrimination? Isn't there some law against it? What's wrong with us brown-haired girls?"

I let her rant a while. I couldn't care less. I'm more concerned about my pants, most of which are starting to feel tight.

"Do you think I look fat?" I ask, unzipping my jeans. I abandon the cheese puffs and check the damage in the full-length mirror on the back of my bedroom door.

"No," says Monica, not even bothering to look up.

"I've already gained ten pounds!"

"So what . . . You're so skinny, no one can tell. Besides, it's all going to your chest anyway."

This, of course, is true, and it's the one thing I really don't mind.

I've always been somewhat flat-chested, but suddenly my breasts have taken on a life all their own. They've nearly doubled in size, and I have cleavage for the first time in my life, which Matt noticed right away. When we're alone, he spends more time talking to my chest than to my face.

"But the doctor says most people only gain three or four pounds the first trimester," I say.

"You're probably filling up on too many empty calories," she says, grabbing the prenatal care book off my desk and thumbing through it. It's become as sacred as the book Carrot Top quotes from and waves in class. I highlight certain passages, and sometimes Monica writes notes in the margins like *Wow—No wonder you're so crabby!* or *Are you getting enough calcium?* "Here it is on page 187," she says. "Make every calorie count. Instead of chips, for example, try a healthier snack such as trail mix or an orange. If that doesn't work, try sublimation. For example, go for a brisk walk or visit an on-line pregnancy chat room . . ."

"*Shut up*," I say, grabbing the book out of her hands. "I need help finding something to wear tonight. All my pants are too tight."

Matt isn't working tonight, so we're going to the football game at school—partly because there's nothing else to do, and partly because I could really go for one of the hot dogs they sell at the concession stand. I've been thinking about hot dogs all day.

"Let's see what you have," Monica says. She starts rummaging through my closet. In less than a minute, she emerges with a black wool skirt with an elastic waist that I haven't worn since freshman year.

"Does this still fit?"

"Probably."

"Great. Let's find something to go with it."

In no time at all, Monica pulls out a fuchsia tank top and a hooded black sweater that zips up the front. They're three pieces that I've had forever, but never thought to wear together.

"Try these," she says.

I look at them uncertainly, but try them on anyway.

"You look fabulous," Monica says.

"You think so?" I have to learn how to take a compliment.

Monica frowns. "It still needs something. You need some cool earrings, something old looking . . ." She looks at her watch. "I need to go. We're doing a family gig again." She rolls her eyes.

"What kind of family gig?" Since everything has happened, it seems as if we talk mostly about me and my life. Monica is my best friend, and I don't even know what's going on with her these days.

Monica smiles gamely and arches her brows. "It's my step-grandmother's birthday, so we're having a party for her. I'm required to stick around until after cake and ice cream. Can you believe it? I don't even know this woman." She groans.

"It doesn't sound that bad."

"Oh yeah? It *will* be bad because Kyle's coming home for the weekend."

"Why don't you meet us at the game afterward?"

"I'll try. If I leave too early, though, my mom will implode."

"So bring Kyle. That way, maybe you can skip out early." I'm half joking, but actually it isn't a bad idea.

Monica looks at me in disgust before leaving. "I think your hormone levels are affecting your brain."

I'm sitting on the floor in my parents' room, sifting through my mother's jewelry box. I borrow jewelry from her all the time, so I know she won't mind.

She still has every piece of jewelry she's ever owned. Some of it's real, but most of it's costume jewelry. She has a lot of vintage hippie gear like beads and chokers and big hoop earrings, plus some of my grandmother's jewelry. I find a pair of dangly gold earrings with an intricate, lacy pattern and pink and purple stones. They look ancient. I study them for a moment and decide they're perfect for tonight's outfit.

I start to put all the jewelry back when I notice a small white envelope at the bottom of the box. It looks old and has yellowed around the edges. I don't remember ever seeing it before. I open the envelope and turn it upside down. A shiny gold locket slips into my palm. This is the first time I've seen *this* piece of jewelry. The locket snaps open easily, and inside is a picture of a baby and a lock of black hair. I never knew Mom kept my baby picture in a locket. I snap the locket shut and notice the inscription on the back—*Forever.* It must have been from Dad. I place it back in the box, along with all the other jewelry I had rummaged through, and close the lid.

Monica shows up during the game's fourth quarter. Matt spots her from the bleachers. "Who's that with her?" Matt asks, waving to get her attention. At first, I think it's some new guy because Monica is the kind of person who actually *could* meet someone four hours after I last saw her. But as they make their way up the bleachers, I realize it's her stepbrother, Kyle.

A group of girls is sitting on the bleachers across from us. They stare at Monica as she makes her way towards us, then clump together and start whispering. This is the standard reaction most girls have to Monica, but it doesn't faze her any more.

Monica and Kyle sit on the bleachers in front of us. There are plenty of seats left now. The visiting team is leading 42 to 20. The bleachers were packed at the start of the game, but most of the crowd left during half time. "Looks like the game's been over for a while," says Kyle, looking at the scoreboard.

"It was over before it started," Matt says, and then smiles for the first time that night.

Monica starts the introductions, but Kyle cuts her off. "I'm Kyle Marsac," he says, cocking his head toward Monica. "The goofball's stepbrother."

Matt laughs. "Matt Ryan."

Matt likes Monica almost as much as I do, but even he thinks her outfits are a little far out at times, and tonight Monica has outdone herself. She's wearing a mini skirt, combat boots, and an authentic army surplus jacket from a thrift store, which I'm pretty sure is all for Kyle's benefit.

Kyle and Matt are in a deep discussion about football when I turn to Monica. "How was the birthday party?"

"Okay. His grandmother is 92 and very hip, but after a while, I was ready to get out of the house."

"Does Kyle know about me?"

"No. I didn't think you were announcing this to the world yet."

"I'm not, but it's okay if you tell him."

She shrugs. "Maybe I will, if I ever talk to him for more than two minutes."

Kyle then looks at me, as if seeing me for the first time that night.

"I like your outfit," he says. "Hey, Monica, you ought to get some fashion advice from your friend here."

I shoot Monica a look. If he only knew . . .

After the game, the four of us stop at Betty's for pizza. Kyle tells us stories about all the campus parties and dorm life at Northwestern. Matt keeps looking at me and squeezing my hand, the way he did when we first met. We can't wait be alone. But Kyle is really funny, and Matt seems to like him. Even Monica is laughing.

"It's great," Kyle says. "A lot different from high school." He looks at me. "So when are you coming to Northwestern for that tour?"

"I don't know." The truth is I haven't given much thought to college lately. It seems too far away. "Maybe after the first of the year."

The waitress brings a large veggie pizza with a stack of plates. "So, if college is so great, why do you come home every weekend?" Monica asks, her voice dripping with sarcasm.

"It's hardly every weekend."

Monica shrugs. "Sure seems like it."

Afterward, Matt and I drive to our usual place to talk. We haven't been back since the day I told him I was pregnant. Tonight, there's a full moon, and the sky is black and starless. Matt parks the car and locks the doors before turning off the engine. We've both had lectures about all the crazy people in the world.

He gives me a slow smile and says, "Alone at last," which is his usual line, but it works. He takes my hand and turns it over, kissing the center of my palm. Then, he kisses me fully on the lips—soft, warm kisses that make my heart pound and my knees go weak. One thing leads to another, and before I know it, we're in the backseat with half of our clothes on the floor of the car. It's the first time we've been together since finding out I was pregnant. He holds me close and whispers, "I love you."

"I love you, too."

"Always?" he asks.

"Always."

And, after that, all I can think is that nothing else matters—not the baby, not school, nothing. Together, we'll work it all out. Everything will be okay. It really will be okay . . . because we love each other.

The next day, Monica and I are both working the afternoon

shift at Java House. For the first two hours, a steady stream of people keeps us so busy there's hardly any time to talk. At one point, the smell of the beans makes me so sick I have to run to the bathroom and puke. The new shift supervisor, who's only 21 and spends the afternoon ogling Monica from the table where he's working, gives me a look when I suddenly leave for the bathroom. A throng of customers is frantic for caffeine, but Monica covers for me. I've gotten it down to the point where I can puke, re-cover, and get back to the counter in five minutes flat.

In the late afternoon, there's finally a lull. It's unseasonably warm today, so Monica props open the front door so we can feel the breeze. We're standing at the counter, looking out the front window, wishing we could be out there. The shift supervisor goes on break, so Monica and I can finally talk.

"Did you and Kyle make it home okay without killing each other?"

"Barely."

"He doesn't seem so bad."

"Yeah, well, he's okay."

"Does that mean you guys have called a truce?"

"Kind of. When we got home, everyone was asleep, so we took two beers and sat on the back porch, drinking and really talking for once. I told him about you. I hope you don't mind."

"I said you could."

"He said that he thought it was really—"

Just then, Niles Sherman walks in with Eyeliner Girl, so I never get to hear what she was about to say. Niles orders a double espresso again, but this time Eyeliner Girl orders an iced vanilla latté. He tells us about a party tonight, but I'm not really up for it, and Monica already has plans with College Boy, whom she's still seeing because she's got nothing better to do. I met him a couple of times. He's really sweet, and he's good to Monica. He calls when he says he will, and he gave her a silver necklace with a heart, which she never wears.

Before they leave, we find out that Eyeliner Girl has a name. "Oh . . . by the way . . . this is Tory," Niles says. She looks up and smiles. "Hi," she says. Her voice is soft. I try to picture her without all that eyeliner.

"You know," Monica says when they leave, "I think Niles is really into her." We stand there watching them while they're still in the parking lot.

Niles and Tory are leaning against the hood of his car, drinking their coffee in the sun. Niles says something to Tory that makes her throw back her head and laugh. Then he leans into her and kisses her forehead.

"I mean, look at them. He was never like that with me."

Just before they head out of the lot, Tory hops off the hood of Nile's car, tosses her cup in the trash three feet away, then starts singing, and does this little dance. With the sun in her hair, she happens to glance my way and wave. And I find myself wishing I could be her. Dancing and singing—with nothing to worry about—the way it used to be.

When I get home, I take a shower and wash my hair twice, trying to get rid of the coffee stench. I smell like one big espresso bean. Later, when I'm in the bathroom drying my hair, Mom comes in. She's wearing a red sweater and jeans. Her hair, as usual, is perfectly coiffed, and she's wearing the diamond studs my father surprised her with for her birthday last year. She leans against the doorjamb and smiles, trying to be casual, but I know something is definitely up.

"I called that couple last night, Ellen and Tom Gardner, the ones who want to adopt a baby," Mom says, crossing her arms in front of her, prepared to do battle.

I don't say anything.

"I know you and Matt haven't made a decision yet, but I

thought that if you met them, it might make your decision easier." She smiles.

I say the safe thing. "Sure."

"Your dad feels you alone need to make the decision, but I believe this is the best way," she says, putting her hand on her hip, ready to lay down the law. "You made a mistake, but there's no reason it has to ruin your entire life. You are only seventeen . . . you're still a child yourself . . ."

"Okay." I don't need another mini lecture. We've been through all this before.

"Anyway, they sound like a very nice couple on the phone, Ali."

"So when do we meet them?"

"Tomorrow."

"*If* I give the baby up for adoption, Matt will want to meet them, too," I say. The truth is, we haven't even talked about it, but I'm sure he'd want to.

"Of course," Mom says. "Dad and I would like to meet them eventually, but if you and Matt want to meet them first, that's fine."

Later, when I tell Matt about the Gardners, he's all for it. We drive to a diner in Joliet, just off the interstate, to meet them the next day. All the way there, I tell Matt I'm open to putting the baby up for adoption, but *only* if we find the right couple. Matt agrees totally.

When we walk into the diner, the Gardners are already waiting for us in a back booth where it's more private. They're both tall and slim.

Ellen Gardner has short, sandy blonde hair, freckles, and blue eyes that crinkle in the corners when she smiles. Tom has brown hair that's starting to recede—and a nice smile.

Tom stands up right away when he sees us. "Hi, you must be Allison and Matt," he says, extending his hand first to me and then to Matt.

"I'm Tom, and this is my wife, Ellen."

"Hi," says Ellen with a big smile. She has really pretty teeth.

Ellen asks us about school and how long Matt and I have known each other. Then there's an awkward silence until a waitress comes to the table. She refills the Gardners' coffee cups and leaves menus.

I don't know what to say, but then Ellen says, "Why don't we tell you both a little about us?"

I didn't *want* to like them, but after two hours at the diner, I have to admit they're really nice. Tom is a business professor at Illinois State University, and Ellen works part-time at a library. They've been married six years and can't have children. They show us pictures of their home, a white two-story house surrounded with flowers, and a picture of their golden retriever named Buddy. They are the perfect couple, with a pretty house and a model dog. All they need is a baby.

We order sandwiches, and Ellen and Tom have a few questions of their own. What subjects do we like at school? Are we willing to disclose our medical histories? How certain are we that we want to give the baby up for adoption? How do our parents feel about it? Some of the questions are easy to answer, some a little harder.

Later, when the waitress clears away our dishes, Ellen leans forward. "We know this is a difficult decision for you to make," she says, "and we understand you need time. But Tom and I want you to know that we're willing to make this an open adoption. If you want to go that route, we'll have our lawyer include that in our legal agreement. After the adoption, we could keep in touch with you, send pictures of the baby. We'll always be honest with our adoptive child. We feel it's important for the baby to know its biological identity."

I get tears in my eyes, and my throat closes. Then Matt says, "Thanks. We'll keep that in mind."

Before leaving the diner, Ellen writes her name and home phone number on the back of Tom's business card.

"Here," she says, handing it to me. "If you think of something you forgot to ask, feel free to call."

"Thanks." Matt and Tom are already outside. Tom is saying something, Matt is nodding his head and smiling, and then they're shaking hands.

Before we leave, Ellen says, "Ali . . . will you call and let us know? Even if you decide to keep the baby?"

"Sure." Then Ellen's eyes start to fill. I want to tell her that the baby is hers, but I can't.

"I'm sorry," Ellen says, wiping her eyes with her fingertips. "I'd probably be a terrible mother anyway." She laughs. "I never have tissues."

"I think you'd be a great mother," I say. I really mean it.

As soon as Matt and I are in the car, he turns to me and says, "They're perfect."

"I know." I look out the car window and watch as the Gardners drive past and wave. I wave back.

"And the thing about the open adoption . . . I think it's a great idea. Don't you?" he asks, pulling onto the interstate. "I mean, this is working out so well."

I stare out the window. It's starting to rain. "Yeah," I say, but he acts as if giving up our baby is the easiest thing. I hate that.

"Ali?" He reaches for my hand, but I pull it away. "What's wrong?" he asks. "Don't tell me you don't like them."

"I like them . . . I'm just not sure."

We drive the rest of the way home in silence.

Chapter 12

When I was in second or third grade, I used to play this game in the car. We'd be driving down the highway, and I thought I could make everything stand still by willing it. Mom, Dad, and I were in the car, frozen in time, while the road and the scenery did all the moving. I didn't realize then that I was reversing my point of view. That's how I feel lately—as if everything's moving and changing so fast. But I'm just standing still.

When I get home from meeting the Gardners, my mother's in the kitchen, waiting at the table with a mug of tea and flipping through a magazine, ready to pump me for information.

"What did you think?"

"What were they like?"

"Isn't this the perfect solution?"

I want to tell her they were horrible freaks and to forget about it, but I can't. I think of Ellen with her blue eyes and Tom with his smile, and I tell her, "They were really great. But I'm still not sure." Then she asks how Matt felt. "He likes them," I say. She gets this smile on her face, and I know she figures the adoption is a done deal.

After dinner, Mom goes into her studio to paint African baskets—her new thing. Dad goes into the den to do paperwork. I try watching TV. *Click. Click. Click.* There's nothing on. I lose myself on-line for a while and then go to bed.

Dad comes into my room and sits on the edge of my bed like he used to do when I was little. He didn't say much about the Gardners tonight at dinner, except that they sounded like good people.

"How's it going?" he asks.

"Not so great," I say. The room is dark, but the moon is full tonight, and it casts a silvery glow on everything. We're both quiet for a long time, and then I say, "I just don't know if giving up my baby is the right choice." He gives me a hug, but doesn't say anything.

"What would you do if you were me? I mean, it's obvious what Mom wants me to do."

"I wish I could tell you what to do, but it's not that simple," he says. "You have to consider each of your options and the pros and cons. I, or your mother, may not weigh all the factors you would. And you're the one who ultimately has to live with the decision."

"But Mom wants me to give the baby up." The tears start coming, so I wipe them away with the corner of a bed sheet.

Dad sighs. "She wants you to continue your education. We both want that, Ali, and I think you want that, too. Right?"

I nod.

"I'm not going to lie to you. Going to college is going to be very tough with a baby. You would be giving up so much—going to school full time, living on a college campus, meeting new people, dating . . . being spontaneous, carefree, and young. Babies require constant care—baths, bottles every few hours or so, diaper changes, not to mention a lot of tender loving care . . . The thing is, I can't tell you what to do. You have to figure it out for yourself, honey." He rubs his eyes and smiles tiredly. "But you don't have to figure it all out tonight. You've had a long day. Get some sleep." Then he kisses the top of my head and says, "You may only be seventeen, Ali, but you're intelligent, and you have a lot of common sense."

Knowing he believes in me should make me feel better, but it doesn't. Not really. I feel like my world is crashing.

On the Monday before Thanksgiving weekend, I stay late to work on my column for the December issue of *The Voice*. It's 4:00, and the school sounds deserted except for the occasional clink of a locker slamming shut. *The Voice* office is a small, narrow glass-enclosed room just off Room 119, where Mrs. Danker teaches journalism. Mrs. Danker is still at her desk grading papers.

For this next issue, everyone turned in their articles early so they wouldn't have to work on them over the long weekend—everyone except for Andy, that is. He's here, writing a recap of the football season. One thing for sure, the story will probably be short. The Warriors won only two games out of eight this year. They ended up at the bottom of the conference standings.

Andy prints out his article and hands it to me. "Here. If you edit it now, I'll make the changes before I leave," he says.

"Wow. I'm impressed. Our deadline's not even until tomorrow morning."

"Don't get used to it, Parker."

"I can hardly wait to read your lead," I say, picking up a blue marker.

Mrs. Danker always lectures us about being objective journalists, but the school board has a problem with any article that doesn't show school spirit.

"Don't worry," he says. "I nailed it."

WARRIORS END DISAPPOINTING SEASON

The varsity football squad had its problems this season. They lost six games, though several were close or last-minute losses . . .

"This is good." I keep reading, circle a few typos, and suggest he change a couple of sentences near the end of his article. Andy makes the changes and gives me a half wave before leaving.

Natalie Halstead is waiting for him in the hall. I've been seeing them together a lot. I never pictured them as a couple, but she's perfect for him: class valedictorian, headed to Dartmouth—she's sure to get in. There was a brief time last year, right before I met Matt, when I was sure Andy was interested in being more than just friends with me. But he never did ask me out, and I'm glad. He's like a brother. If he'd asked me out, it would have ruined everything.

I try to refocus on my work so I can leave, too. The cursor on the computer screen pulses impatiently. It's a real effort to get back into the column I'd been working on about the pop machines in school. The school board wants to remove them from campus, but someone started a petition in opposition, and everyone's signing it. Usually, I like writing about controversial topics like this, but tonight I can barely string two sentences together. I think I have writer's block. I think I should reconsider a career in journalism. Mrs. Danker comes in and saves me before I completely self-destruct.

"Oh, Allison, you're still here," she says. Mrs. Danker is a heavy-set woman with dark brown hair threaded with gray.

"Hi," I say, glancing at the clock on the wall. "Actually, I'm just finishing up. I have most of the copy for you." I hand her a stack. "I'll get the rest to you tomorrow before class."

"Looks like you've been busy," she says, sitting down in the chair next to me. "Do you have a few minutes?"

"Sure." Sometimes Mrs. Danker wants to discuss future issues of *The Voice* or an idea for an article. So I don't think anything of it, but then she hesitates, and all of a sudden, I know this isn't an impromptu planning session.

"I was wondering if everything is okay. You're maintaining an A in my class, but you've been tardy a few times, and you seem to have lost a little of your enthusiasm as editor."

I have a half smile on my face, wishing I could just disappear. I don't want to talk with her about it. "I, uh . . . well, I've been having some personal problems." I look at her briefly and then start fiddling with a paper clip.

"Is there anything I can do to help?" Mrs. Danker asks.

"I don't think so."

"Ali, we have a special counselor who comes here three times a week to help students sort out personal problems. Her name is Audrey Connor. She's great," she says, "and anything you tell her is completely confidential." Before leaving, she writes Ms. Connor's name and phone number on a slip of paper.

"Thanks."

"You're quite welcome."

⤚✦⤙

The day before Thanksgiving, my mother is having a minor breakdown over a ten-pound turkey. She's forty-seven years old, and she's never actually cooked a whole turkey before. That's because our Thanksgivings are usually spent in Indiana. Grandma Jeanne makes the turkey, and the aunts and uncles bring everything else. My mother suggests we stay home this year because of my, ahem, "situation," which is fine by me. We haven't told anyone on Dad's side of the family, and I'm not up for all the questions. It's not that we're planning to keep it a secret, but I know everyone will be asking me about next year and which colleges I've applied to. Three months ago, I knew what I wanted, but now, I'm not sure what's going to happen.

My mother's on the phone with the turkey hotline people, whom she called 15 minutes ago, and she's still taking notes. My father stands in the kitchen looking helpless, hands jammed in his pockets. "There will only be the four of us," he says. "Why don't we make reservations somewhere?"

My mother glares at him, covers the phone, and hisses, *"We are not eating restaurant turkey!"*

Aunt Laura comes by Thanksgiving morning, bringing a store-bought pumpkin pie and big purple chrysanthemums. Mom's turkey comes out of the oven dry, but that's easy to fix. We drench it with the gravy my dad found in a jar at Vincent's Market, after my mother burned the gravy she was trying to make from scratch. After eating, I place a hand on my stomach. In the past couple weeks, I've developed a bulge. It's small and firm, but it's still not that obvious, especially when I wear loose sweaters and shirts.

Later, we go for a walk at a park near our house, and when we get back, the phone is ringing. It's Matt, so I head upstairs. I've been wanting to talk with him all day, but things between us have changed. On the phone, we don't talk and joke around the way we used to. Everything is centered on the future . . . the baby, college, what we're going to do. It seems like we're always arguing. Lately, it's just like dealing with my mother.

When we hang up, I go downstairs. My aunt is getting ready to leave, and my mom and dad are standing in the entryway. My purple overnight bag is next to the front door.

"What's up?" I ask.

"I'm kidnapping you," says my aunt.

"Your father and I think it would be good for you to get away for a couple of days," says Mom. "We think you need time to just . . ."

"Okay," I say, which surprises everyone, including myself. Nine months ago, when Matt and I first started dating, I wouldn't have *considered* spending an entire weekend without him. But there's so much tension lately. It'll be a relief to get away.

"I was hoping you'd want to," Aunt Laura says, smiling. "I thought maybe we'd go shopping for maternity clothes."

On Friday, Aunt Laura takes me to this great maternity store on Oak Street that her pregnant friend told her about. When I see the prices, I think we should go someplace else, but Aunt Laura tells me it's her treat, and helps me pick out a pair of maternity jeans, a sweater, a denim mini skirt, a pair of black pants, and a couple of tops to go with them.

When we get back to her apartment, she makes hot chocolate from scratch, the one thing she's really good at. My aunt's apartment is amazing. Her furniture is all cream leather, faux fur rugs, and glass tabletops. Everything is neutral except the bright oversized prints on the walls. I'm sitting on the sofa in her living room, checking out the view of Lake Michigan, thinking this is exactly the sort of place where I'd like to live someday, when she hands me a mug.

"Thanks, again, for everything. I love the jeans." I haven't been this excited about a pair of jeans since I was thirteen. I put them on almost as soon as we walked in the door. The front panel is expandable and much more comfortable than my regular jeans. I figure that if I wear them with oversized sweaters, no one will even guess I'm pregnant.

"What's it like?" she asks, sitting down next to me.

"Strange. It's like having an alien inhabit your body. I'm tired all the time, and I still feel sick sometimes, but I've gained fifteen pounds anyway. And I'm starting to show." I pull my sweater up just far enough to bare my stomach. It's nice having someone ask about me. Most everybody just talks about the future.

Aunt Laura takes a sip of her hot chocolate and looks out the window. "I wish this were happening to me and not you," she says.

"Me, too," I say, and we both laugh. Sometimes, life seems unfair. Take the Gardners, for instance. Ellen told me they tried having a baby for years. Years! The first time Matt and I do it without a condom, I get pregnant.

As if reading my mind, Aunt Laura says, "Kate told me about the Gardners."

"They're really nice. When I met them, it was like we'd always known each other."

"It sounds like you're seriously considering adoption. Have you considered anyone other than the Gardners?"

"No," I say, but then it occurs to me that Aunt Laura might want to adopt my baby. No, that'd be too weird. But I wonder if this is what this weekend is really all about. "I don't know what to do," I say. "I don't even want to think about it. Mostly, I just think about this baby and whether it'll be a boy or a girl, what it'll look like, what it'll be like. And I try to imagine how I'll feel knowing a part of me is out there, away from me."

"One thing's for sure," says Aunt Laura. "Your baby will be beautiful. You were the most beautiful baby I'd ever seen. You had this gorgeous red-gold hair."

There are only a few pictures of me from when I was first born, and in all of them, I'm wearing a pink cap or my hair looks really dark. I remember the locket I found in my mother's jewelry box.

"I think my hair was black at first," I say. "In fact, I know it was. I found a locket the other day in Mom's jewelry box. Inside, there's a baby picture of me and a lock of black hair."

Aunt Laura is quiet. She sets her mug on the coffee table and curls her legs under her on the cream leather sofa. "No, Allison, I remember quite clearly because I was there the day you were born. Your hair was reddish-gold."

The next afternoon, Mom picks me up at the train station in Lakeview.

"How was your weekend?"

"Great."

"Looks like you did some shopping," she says, eyeing the packages in the backseat.

"Aunt Laura took me to this great maternity shop on Oak Street."

I'm quiet for a while, and then I ask the one question that's been on my mind all weekend. "Mom, what about Aunt Laura? Do you think she wants to adopt my baby?" In some ways, it could be ideal, but I'm not sure how I feel about it.

"I admit, it did cross my mind . . . Laura's too . . . but we agreed it wouldn't be right. It's not fair to you, and it's not fair to the baby. And we both agreed it would make it harder for you to move on with your life."

I feel relieved. I don't think I'd like it either. We're almost home when I remember the conversation I had with Aunt Laura yesterday afternoon.

"Mom?"

"Yes."

"Aunt Laura and I were talking about babies this weekend and what mine would look like . . . I was wondering what color my hair was when I was born."

"It was reddish-gold," she says, turning to me. She smiles. "Everyone commented on what an unusual shade it was."

"Oh," I say, immediately wondering who the baby in the locket was.

One thing for sure, it wasn't me. I glance at my mom to ask her about it, but she's looking for a list she misplaced in her purse and almost runs a stop light. I point out that if I almost ran a stop light, I'd be hearing about it for days.

Then we get into an argument, I forget all about the locket, and by the time we get home, we're not speaking again.

Chapter 13

In English class, we start *Hamlet*, Carrot Top's personal favorite. Lucky for us, she found the original uncut version, which is something like four thousand lines. "After Jesus," she says, "Hamlet is the most quoted figure in Western culture." She pauses for a moment to let this sink in, as if we care. Then she gets teary and dabs at her eyes with a tissue.

Monica slips me a note: "I HATE THIS SHAKESPEARE CRAP." While I'm reading it, Carrot Top marches towards me and confiscates it, which gets Monica one-on-one time with Carrot Top after class. So after class, instead of leaving with Monica, I walk out with Niles, who shows me his latest tattoo. Next to the star on his left wrist is one word: Tory.

In second period study hall, Matt's in a good mood, so we're talking and joking around before class the way we used to. I ask him if he's seen Niles' new tattoo. "Yeah," he says. "He's really into Tory. They're intense." Neither of us brings up the baby or the Gardners. When the bell rings, he slips me a Jolly Rancher— watermelon (my favorite). After class, he asks if I want to skip the cafeteria today to get a taco for lunch, but I can't. I'd set up a meeting with Ms. Connor.

"Do you want to come with me?" I ask him.

He shrugs. "Maybe next time."

In business class, Mr. Fitz lectures about inventory control. He drones on about FIFO and LIFO . . . First In First Out . . . Last In First Out. My brain shifts into autopilot. I open my notebook and start doodling hearts. The guy next to me puts his head on his book and falls asleep in two seconds. At first, I don't think he's really sleeping, but his mouth is open, and he's starting to drool.

After business class, I grab a veggie sandwich in the cafeteria and eat it on my way to Ms. Connor's office. This is my second appointment with her. I met with her the first time earlier this week. Ms. Connor has long dark hair and looks younger than most of the teachers at Lakeview. She wears long print skirts, boots, and a lot of ethnic jewelry. She keeps a jar of lemon drops on her desk. At the first appointment, I ate five lemon drops, one after another. I wasn't even sure I'd tell her I was pregnant. But, then we started talking, and somewhere along the way, it just came out.

"So how are things going?" Ms. Connor asks. I'm in her office, which is so tiny there's room only for a desk and two chairs. Her office is at the end of a corridor near the chemistry labs. I've walked past it countless times, but never noticed it before.

"Pretty good."

"Where should we start today?"

"I dunno."

"Well, how about your boyfriend—Matt, right? What's he like?"

Just the mention of his name makes me smile. "Matt's not like most guys . . ." I want to explain this isn't some high school crush. It's The Real Thing. I mean, I could be in a room with 100 guys, and I'd be drawn to Matt. "He's different."

"How is he different?" Ms. Connor asks.

All of a sudden, my mind goes blank. "He's funny . . . he makes me laugh . . . and he's been supportive about all this." Not at first, but I don't tell Ms. Connor that. That's in the past.

"How does he feel about the pregnancy?"

"He was shocked at first. He wanted me to have an abortion, but I couldn't." I look down and study my shoes. "He thinks we should give the baby up for adoption."

"How do you feel about that?"

It's been on my mind a lot lately. I know I need to make a decision. "I guess adoption is the only way, but . . . I don't know."

"Why are you reluctant?" Ms. Connor asks.

"I don't know if I can carry a baby for nine months and then give it away."

"Do you want to keep the baby?"

"Part of me wants to, yes," I say, and for some reason I start to cry.

Ms. Connor hands me a box of tissues. "Ali, before you were pregnant, did you ever think about what your life after high school would be like?"

"Sure."

"What was it going to be like?" she asks.

"I was planning to go to college full time, get a degree in journalism, and then work for a newspaper or maybe a TV station."

"Have you thought about what would happen if you kept the baby?"

I shrug and study the jar of lemon drops on her desk.

"This baby may push your goals and dreams aside," she says. "Are you prepared for that to happen?"

"I don't know."

Ms. Connor pulls out some books and brochures from a cabinet near her desk. I notice a few pictures on the shelf behind her desk. They're all of a little girl with dark, curly hair. She looks about three years old. "There's a lot you need to think about," she says. "I'll be honest with you. It'll be hard to go to college full time and care for a baby. Babies need constant attention. And if you had planned to live in a dorm on campus, that'll be impossible."

"I know."

"Have you considered the costs involved?"

"A little." I pop a lemon drop into my mouth and bite down hard. The fact is, I haven't thought about the costs at all. All things considered, they don't seem that relevant to me right now.

"There are so many things you'll need—diapers, formula, clothes, medicine, medical care. You also need to consider the cost of rent if you plan to live away from home, and factor in day care expenses and tuition. Of course, you may get help from your parents, your boyfriend, maybe even his parents. But you need to find out now what they're willing and able to provide, and whether it's in the form of money or hands-on help with the baby. You have a lot to think through."

Ms. Connor hands me a stack of books and brochures. "What I want you to do is make two lists. On the first one, list the pros and cons of keeping your baby. On the second, I want you to list the pros and cons of adoption. Okay?"

"Okay."

"Let's meet again next Monday and go over your lists." Ms. Connor opens her appointment book. "Shall we meet during lunch again?"

"Sure." I shove the books in my backpack. "Is that your daughter in the pictures?" I ask.

Ms. Connor pulls one of the frames down from a shelf. She smiles. "Yes. Her name is Zoe."

"She's cute," I say.

Ms. Connor smiles. "Thanks . . . She's a handful." I wonder about Ms. Connor. She doesn't wear a wedding ring, and there are no pictures of a Mr. Connor in sight.

When I open the door to the hallway, Kelly, the senior I saw at Planned Parenthood the first time I was there, is leaning against the wall.

"Hi," I say, wondering if Kelly is there for the same reason.

"Hi," she says, and looks away.

Just then Ms. Connor steps out of her office.

"Kelly, hi. Sorry to keep you waiting," Ms. Connor says. I'm halfway down the hall when I hear the door to her office close. Kelly could be there for any reason—any reason at all. Still, I didn't miss the fact that she's wearing a Chicago Bulls sweatshirt, size extra large.

❧

"Do you think she's pregnant?" Monica asks.

"I don't know for sure," I say. I called Monica right after getting home from school. "Kelly could have been there for any reason." I wish I hadn't said anything. I hate the idea of everyone talking about me behind my back at school, and I know they already are. It's pretty hard to conceal my stomach in the locker room, where there's no privacy. Some of the girls are already starting to guess. I see them staring at my waist and whispering. I have to get out of P.E. somehow.

"Did she look pregnant?" Monica asks.

"I don't know . . . It's hard to tell." I don't mention the over-sized sweatshirt.

"Anyway, what's going on with you?" I ask. I still feel bad because all we talk about is me. *Me, me, me.* Even *I'm* bored talking only about me.

"Well. . ."

I can tell by the tone of her voice that something is definitely up. "What?"

"I went out with someone new over Thanksgiving."

"And you didn't tell me? Who?"

"Kyle."

"Your brother?"

"*Step*brother," Monica says, putting the emphasis on "step."

"Whoa."

"You're the one who was always so high on him, you know," Monica says, defensively.

"I know. He's a great guy . . ."

"But?"

"I'm just surprised. I mean, he's your brother, Mon—"

"*Step*brother."

"So . . . where'd you go?"

"A movie."

"And . . . ?"

"And afterwards, we were sitting in his car, letting the engine warm up, and he gave me this look. I said 'what?' and he said, 'you,' and then he leaned over and kissed me."

"Just like that?"

"Just like that."

"I thought you couldn't stand him."

Monica laughs. "We're getting along much better now."

"Your mom must be freaking."

"No kidding. She and Steve would be hysterical, so we're not telling them. They just think we're getting along."

"Wow, Monica . . . I don't know what to say."

"I thought you'd be happy for me."

"I just hope you know what you're doing."

"I'm seeing someone whom I think is . . . very special."

"Who *also* happens to be your stepbrother."

"You make it more complicated than it is."

"Mon?"

"Yeah?"

"It *is* complicated."

ஃ

The next morning, Mom drives me to Dr. Bishop's office for my monthly checkup. I hate these visits. Everyone stares, silently clucking their tongues and shaking their heads. It's hard to blend in when the majority of the women in the waiting room are in their thirties, drive Volvo station wagons, and wear wedding rings. At the clinic, at least there were girls my age.

When the nurse calls me, I follow her into an examining room. Mom stays in the waiting area. The nurse checks my weight and blood pressure, then asks me to pee in a cup so she can make sure my sugar and protein levels are okay. The nurse leaves me in the examining room, and a few minutes later, Dr. Bishop walks in carrying my chart.

"How are you doing?" she asks.

"Fine."

"Well, it certainly looks that way. Your weight is good, blood pressure too . . ." she says, looking over my chart. "Have you felt the baby move yet?"

I shake my head. "Should I be worried?"

Dr. Bishop is quick to smile. "You should feel something any day now. Why don't you lie down so we can see how you're doing."

Dr. Bishop measures my stomach and then uses a special instrument to listen for the baby's heartbeat. "There it is," she says. *Lub, dub, lub, dub, lub, dub*. As soon as I hear it, the tears start coming. And as weird as it may seem, that's when the reality of it all hits me. *I'm having a baby. I'm really having a baby.* It's amazing—it really is.

Later that night, I'm lying on my bed, leaning against a pillow. I have a yellow legal pad and my favorite blue pen in front of me. Like a good little girl, I'm making my lists for Ms. Connor. The list of cons for keeping the baby goes on and on and on. No surprise there. I'm only seventeen. I have no job. No money. No home of my own. I don't know anything about babies. I want to go to college and live in a dorm. Matt doesn't want this baby. I have only one entry under pros—I want my baby.

Why wouldn't I? It's in my body for nine months. It's a part of me. But when I look at the list, I realize the most logical choice is to give the baby to the Gardners.

I toss my notepad on the floor and flop back on the pillow. I feel a twinge—just the slightest feeling—like wings flapping inside.

I sit very still, hoping to feel it again, but nothing happens. Then, just when I think I must have imagined it, it happens again.

I lay a hand on my stomach and rub it. "Hey, how are you do-ing in there?" I can't help but smile. "I'm your mom." At least, I think I want to be.

❦

The first thing Ms. Connor asks me on Monday is whether I finished my lists. I tell her I'm still working on them, which is totally untrue. Since I don't have the lists, Ms. Connor suggests we talk about my options and my personal goals. Before I leave, she gives me more information on prenatal care and adoption. She also gives me this book about girls who decided to raise their babies on their own.

"Don't forget to work on those lists, Ali," she calls after me. Whatever.

We've decided to meet twice a week now, usually at lunch-time. During one of our meetings, Ms. Connor says I should tell my teachers I'm pregnant. At first, I don't want to. It's not any of their business, and being pregnant has not affected my brain. I can still write 500-word essays, take tests, and edit *The Voice*, thank you very much. But Ms. Connor insists, so I do it, partly because I like her and partly because I want to get her off my back. It goes easier than I expected, and everyone's fine about it, except for my business teacher, Mr. Fitz, who's a jerk.

I was feeling really bad one morning, so, as usual, I'd brought saltines to class, but Mr. Fitz told me that eating was not allowed in his classroom and there would be no exceptions, not even for me. So I ran out of his class to throw up. The next day, Ms. Connor pulled him aside, and now he overlooks my crackers, but shoots me disapproving looks every other opportunity he gets.

After school, Monica comes over to my house to hang out for a while. I'm eating cookie dough ice cream directly from a carton and checking out my profile in my bedroom mirror while Monica reads from the prenatal book.

"Let's see," she says. "Month four . . . fatigue, constipation, headaches, increased appetite."

"*Shut up* . . . Isn't there anything to *look forward to* this month?"

She looks up for a second, then turns back to the book and mumbles to herself. After a few minutes, she says, "Here it is . . . end to nausea and vomiting, decreased urinary frequency, and continued breast enlargement."

"Well, *that's* more like it," I say, scraping the last of the ice cream from the carton. "You know . . . Andy was looking at me funny today . . . Do you think he's guessed? Because I really don't thinks it's *that obvious*, do you?"

Monica looks up. "*Duh*," she says, which kind of hurts my feelings, even though I don't say so.

But Monica knows me too well, and her voice softens. "Look, Ali, I'm sorry, but *get real*. Either you're pregnant or you swallowed a very small pumpkin."

Chapter 14

The second Saturday of December is the day my father searches for the perfect Christmas tree. And my mother, who hates to bake, insists we make cookies because of something I said when I was five years old that I don't remember. The story goes like this: My mother and I are baking Christmas cookies together. I'm only five and insist on doing everything myself. There's flour everywhere, the kitchen is a wreck, and my mother is feeling *really, really* grouchy, when I look up and tell her this is the best day of my life. Thus began a family tradition.

This Saturday is no different. I wake up, pull on some clothes, and find my mom in the kitchen with all the baking stuff lined up on the counter ready to go. My dad's already left to get the tree. I'm making some toast, and my mom's at the kitchen table, reading the morning paper and drinking coffee as she always does. "Niles Sherman," she says. "Isn't he a friend of Matt?"

"Yeah," I say, taking a bite of toast.

"He was in a car accident last night," she says, still reading. "Three passengers were with him. Two were killed."

"What?" I'm thinking there must be some mistake, but I sit in the chair across from her and she hands me the paper so I can read it myself.

TWO TEENS DIE FROM LAKEVIEW CRASH

A sixteen-year-old girl from North View High School became the second teen to die after a crash Friday night,

*when a speeding car carrying her and three others ca-
reened out of control . . . Tory Bloom died late Friday
night at St. Mary's Hospital. Her friend, Jenna Kingsley,
died on impact. The driver, Niles Sherman, and another
passenger, Nick Pedraza, suffered minor injuries . . .
The car was traveling west on Lakeview Avenue at a high
speed when the car spun out of control.*

Mom puts a hand on my shoulder as I finish reading the
article. "It's such a shame," she says. "Those kids are so young
. . . and Niles . . ."

She shakes her head. "How will he live with this the rest of
his life?"

I sit there stunned, trying to process what I just read.

"Ali . . . are you all right? Did you know all these kids?"

"Yeah . . . Niles and Nick, yes, and Tory, well sort of . . . I
didn't know Jenna."

I picture Tory and Niles the last time they were at the coffee
shop. I can see Tory in the parking lot, singing and dancing, the
sun shining off her hair. It's hard to imagine she's dead. Though I
met Tory only twice, I feel like I knew her. On the front page of
the newspaper, there's a picture of her, looking right at me, looking so alive. It's hard to imagine she's gone. Just like that. Dead.

I call Matt right away. He's getting ready to leave for work.
He didn't know. "I'll call you later," he says. Then Monica calls,
and we talk for an hour. I didn't know them well, except for Niles,
but I can't get it out of my mind all day.

My mom asks if we should just forget baking, but for some
reason, I want to keep busy. So we roll out cookie dough, cut out
shapes, and put them in the oven just as we always do. I tell Mom
about the day Niles came into the Java House with Tory—how they
drank their coffee in the parking lot, and how Tory started singing
and did this dance. I tell her how Niles tattooed Tory's name on
the inside of his wrist. And then we talk about how short life is

and how everything can change so fast.

Then my dad comes home with the tree. "This is the best one yet," he says, dragging it through the back door, the house filling with the scent of pine. My mom tells him what happened, and he drops everything to read the story. Even though he never met Niles or Tory or any of the others, I can tell the news really affects him. Later, while I'm frosting cookies, he kisses the top of my head and stands there watching me, as if I'm going to disappear any second.

Later, he goes out to the garage to look for Christmas lights. Mom and I start to clean up the kitchen when I remember about the locket.

"There's something I've been meaning to ask you."

"What?" Mom asks.

"I found this locket in your jewelry box with a picture of a baby and a lock of black hair, and I was wondering . . ."

"Whether it was you?" Mom's face goes white. She picks up a dish towel and wipes her hands slowly. Then she sits down on a stool next to the kitchen counter. "Ali . . . there's something I need to tell you. I should have told you a long time ago." She looks out the kitchen window.

It's starting to snow.

"I had a baby when I was nineteen."

"*You* . . . had a baby? *You?*"

"Yes."

"Why didn't you tell me?"

"I don't know . . ." She shakes her head. "It happened so long ago . . . it was water under the bridge, and I'd spent so many years shutting it out. When you told me you were pregnant, it was all so painful for me, like I was reliving my own first time."

"What happened?"

"I gave him up . . . It was hard . . . but it was for the best."

Everything's so clear now. "I get it. You think *I* should give up the baby because that's what *you* did."

"I was too young to take care of a baby . . ."

"So you took the easy way out."

"Don't talk to me like that, young lady," Mom snaps. "If you want to be treated like an adult, start acting like one."

"I *am* trying to act like an adult, but you won't let me. You want to make all my decisions, and you don't care how I feel! How could you do it? How could you give your baby away?"

Mom slaps me across the face, something she's never done before. I can't believe it. I touch my cheek—it's burning—and all I can think is that I have to get out of there. I fling open the kitchen door and leave. I have no idea where I'm going, but I'm going there as fast as I can. I walk six blocks, and my sides are starting to ache, but I don't care. I just keep on going.

Later, when I come back, I find Dad in the kitchen, cleaning up the mess from our baking session.

"Where's Mom?"

"She went out for a while. Are you okay? Your mom told me what happened."

I shrug and start to walk away.

"Allison."

"Yes?"

Dad looks at me for a long moment. "Maybe your mom should have told you sooner, but it was her decision not to. Don't judge her too harshly."

Mom comes home an hour later. I'm in my room upstairs, but I hear my parents talking in low voices downstairs. I'm sure Mom will come up to talk with me, but she doesn't, which isn't like her at all. Dad said I was judging her. Maybe I was, but I feel as if she's lied to me all these years.

I find Mom in her studio. Her bifocals are sitting low on her nose, the way she wears them when she's working. When I walk in, she takes off her glasses, and smiles, fatigue in her eyes. "I was about to come looking for you." Her eyes are red and watery.

"Mom, I'm sorry . . ."

She raises her hand. "No, Allison, I'm sorry. I never should have slapped you, and I should have told you sooner about the baby I had. Your dad wanted me to. He felt it would help you deal with things now. I never wanted you to know . . .

"Everything was so different then," she continues, a faraway look in her eyes. "It was very hush-hush. Grandma and Grandpa were very religious, and my pregnancy was a disgrace to them. They didn't want the neighbors to know, so I was sent to a convent that took in unwed mothers. I was three months pregnant."

"What happened?"

She smiles. "I had a little boy. The doctor told me he weighed more than eight pounds. I don't know who adopted him. I was in a labor room by myself across from the nursery. Right after the baby was born, they took him away. No one thought I should see him. Apparently, that's how it was done in those days. Fortunately, one nurse came to check on me and really listened to what I was going through. She understood how desperately I needed closure."

Mom's eyes are bordered with tears, but she doesn't bother to brush them away. "The nurse brought him to me late one night. I held him in my arms for an hour, and I told him goodbye. That was the first and last time I ever saw him. The nurse took a picture of him for me. That's the picture you saw."

I swallow hard. "Who was the father?"

"A boy on campus I met the first week of school. We dated for a few months, and I was so in love with him. He gave me the locket with the inscription. I thought he loved me, but he walked completely away from it and pretended it never happened."

"Does Dad know?"

"Of course."

"Why didn't you ever tell me?"

"I don't know, Ali. I always planned to, but sometimes it's hard to point out your mistakes to your children. When you and Matt started spending so much time together, I thought of telling you. I know you think I dislike Matt, but I never had a problem with him. It's just that whenever I saw the two of you together, it reminded me of my own experience, and I was worried you were getting too serious. I didn't want you to make the same mistake I made."

"Did you ever try to find him—your baby, I mean?"

"No, I didn't think it would be fair to him or his parents. And now," she shrugs, "he's a grown man."

It's hard to imagine. My mother's not the kind of person who makes mistakes. She's the woman with the perfectly coiffed hair, and the right lipstick always in place. "There's one thing I don't get," I say.

"What's that?" Mom asks.

"If you had your baby, why were you pushing me to get an abortion?"

"Temporary insanity, I guess." She shakes her head. "I don't completely understand it myself. At the time, I really believed an abortion was the best option for you. Giving up my baby was the hardest thing I've ever done. I didn't want you to go through that kind of pain . . . Not a day goes by that I don't think about him."

Just then I feel a twinge, and without thinking, I place a hand on my stomach. It feels funny, like having a goldfish swimming inside.

"Is the baby moving?" Mom asks.

I take Mom's hand and rest it on my stomach, and almost immediately there's another ripple. "Oh, I feel it. He must be very strong," she says. Then, we're both laughing and crying all at once.

"Or she," I say.

"Or she," Mom agrees. "It's amazing, isn't it? Being pregnant?"

"Mom . . ."

"Hmm?"

"I want to keep the baby."

Mom doesn't say anything for a long while, and I wonder what she's thinking. Here she is, the mother I've known all my life, with a past she completely hid from me. All of a sudden, she looks different somehow. Suddenly, she isn't just my mother. She's this woman who once fell in love with someone who wasn't my dad.

"I can't carry this baby for nine months and then give it up. I just can't."

Mom starts to cry all over again. "Okay," she says finally. Then she takes me in her arms and holds me, and we cry. It feels good, leaning into her like that. I haven't felt this close to my mother in a very long time.

Dad's in the den working on some papers when I tell him. "It won't be easy," he says.

"I know."

"And I want you to continue your education, just as you've always planned. Your mom and I will help you as much as we can with the baby, but I don't want you giving up your dreams."

"I won't—I promise." I've been thinking of taking a year off from school, but I'll talk to my parents about that later.

I start to walk away when Dad says, "Allison . . ."

"Yeah?"

"You should let the Gardners know. It's only fair."

"Can you do that, Dad?" I can't.

He thinks about it a minute. My parents are big on having me handle my own problems. "Sure," he finally says. "But if you change your mind about keeping the baby, that's okay, too. Your mom and I will support your decision either way."

"Thanks, but I'm not going to change my mind." My determination is now like a rock inside me.

That night in my room, I feel the baby move again. "Hey,"
I say, resting my hand on my stomach. "We're going to stick to-
gether, okay? So, you're going to need a name." I have a list of
baby names I like in a journal I've kept since elementary school.
My favorite girl name used to be Shana—Shana Nicole. But now it's
Willow, which is the name of a character I read about in a book
last spring for English class. So maybe I could name her Willow
Shana . . . or Willow Nicole. My favorite boy's name is Jordan, and
I've always liked Matt's name, too. I put my hand on my stomach
and try it out in my head. *Jordan Matthew Ryan.*

"I'm keeping my baby," I tell Matt the next day when he gets
off work. He works every Sunday now from 8:00 until 3:00. Just to
be sure I wouldn't miss him, I came by a half hour early. I never
call his house any more when I know his parents are home. Matt
sits there, on the hood of his car.

"*Our* baby," he says.

I look at him and smile. "Whatever . . ." I say. "Anyway, Matt,
there are some things I need to—"

"No, Ali, not '*whatever,*'" Matt says. "I'm sick and tired of
this only being about you!"

"I'm sorry . . ."

"No, Ali, you're not sorry. You don't even get it! *I'm* the baby's father, but that doesn't mean anything to you. You've been
pushing me away since day one. You don't tell me you're pregnant
for weeks, then you decide *not* to have an abortion without con-
sulting me. And now, you've come to tell me you're keeping *your*
baby." He laughs a short, harsh laugh.

His cheeks are red, the way they always get when he's upset, and that muscle in his face is twitching again. "What do you
think I am, Ali? Some robot?" There are tears in his eyes, and his

voice is thick with emotion. "I realize I was not exactly the stellar boyfriend at first, okay? I was shocked. And as corny as it sounds, I never thought we would have to deal with this. I thought this couldn't possibly happen to us. We were invincible. But guess what? It did. And I'm trying to help, but you keep pushing me away."

He opens the car door and slams it shut in one swift movement. "You think I don't care about you or the baby? I love you. Okay? I love you!" he yells. He turns the key in the ignition, revs up the engine, and roars away.

⁂

The stereo is cranked up, and as I make the loop that Monica and I always take, I think about what Matt said. When I get home, I see Matt's car parked down the street from my house, engine idling. I pull my mom's car into the garage and run down the street. All I can hear is the crunch of the snow under my feet. He's standing there, leaning against the hood, waiting for me, his breath coming out in small, white puffs.

"I'm sorry," I say. "You're right."

"I'm sorry, too."

He reaches out and holds me tight, and for a while, we don't say anything. I'm thinking about the car accident and how everything in life can change so fast. And how what's happening to us might not be the most awful thing in the world.

"I keep thinking of Niles," I say, "and Tory . . . and . . ."

"I know," he says. "I know." Looking me in the eyes, he says, "We can handle this . . . We can."

And suddenly, I feel so calm, so sure—something I haven't felt for months.

Chapter 15

Niles Sherman isn't at school on Monday, and neither is Nick Pedraza. A major story about the accident was on the front page of the local paper, and everyone is talking about it. Apparently, the street was slick, Niles was driving too fast, and the car spun out of control. It slammed into a light pole, and the back of the car was crushed. Tory died from head injuries, and the other girl, who it turns out was her best friend, died on impact. The accident is still under investigation, though drugs and alcohol were not involved. Niles is in a lot of trouble because he wasn't supposed to be driving—his license was still under suspension. A candlelight vigil at North View High is going to take place for Tory and Jenna on Wednesday.

Matt's late to study hall, so when he sits down, I slip him a note: "How's Niles?"

He writes back: "Not good. He's really taking it hard."

Maybe it's morbid, but I can't stop thinking of the accident. I keep wondering what they were doing that night. Where were they going? What were they talking about? The paper said they were on their way to get something to eat, but then after study hall, Matt tells me they were really on their way to a party. A friend of Tory was having a big bash at his parents' house. And the other girl, Jenna Kingsley, didn't even know Niles and Nick. She'd just met them that night.

I have an appointment to see Ms. Connor at lunch again. I don't really feel up to it. At first we talk about the accident—how sad it is and how accidents can happen. I eat seven lemon drops, one after another, biting down hard every time. Then she asks how things are going, as she always does, so I tell her everything—the stuff with my mom, the blowup with Matt, and my decision.

Ms. Connor considers it all, studying the notepad that rests on her lap, as she usually does while I'm talking, but when I tell her that Mom gave her baby up for adoption, she looks up.

"How do you feel about that?"

"Well, Grandma and Grandpa made it very hard for her, but there's this part of me that still thinks it's wrong to give your baby away."

"Why?"

"I don't know . . . It's your baby."

"Is it right to keep it if you can't give it a home or take care of it?"

"I guess not."

"Allison, there's no right or wrong decision. You make the best decision you can at the place where you are. It sounds to me like that's what your mom did."

Maybe Ms. Connor is right. Grandma and Grandpa made it impossible for Mom to keep her baby.

"Now," says Ms. Connor, "tell me more about Matt's reaction to all this."

I tell her about our conversation yesterday. I've been think-ing about it a lot. All this time, I've been so busy thinking about how I feel—how Matt couldn't begin to understand what it's like to be me. Never once did it occur to me what it must be like to be him.

"Have you and Matt discussed what responsibilities you will share once the baby arrives?"

"No. We haven't . . . uh . . . gotten that far yet."

"You'll need to at some point. It sounds like he wants to be a part of this baby's life. He's more than welcome to make an appointment with me, too." Ms. Connor takes a book off her shelf. "In the meantime, give this to Matt," she says, handing me a book for teenage fathers. "By the way, have you considered what last name you will give your baby?"

"Uh . . . not really." When I was thinking of baby names, I automatically used Ryan as the last name, but I haven't talked with Matt about it yet, so I'm still not sure.

"Well, that's something you may need to check into. I assume that you and the baby will be covered under your parents' health insurance?"

"I think so." Once I made my decision, Dad said he would check on it.

"You'll want your mom or dad to look into it. Under some health plans, the baby must have the same last name as its mother to qualify for coverage."

Details. Details. Details.

"Oh, Ali, one more thing. There's another girl at school who's pregnant. She's due in April. I thought maybe you two would like to start meeting here, together, after the holidays."

"Sure." I wonder if she's talking about Kelly. I wouldn't mind talking with someone who's going through the same thing. Besides, it isn't like it's a secret any more.

<hr/>

"I already called the insurance company," Dad says that night when I ask him about insurance coverage. "You're covered under my health plan. As far as the baby is concerned, all we have to do is file an affidavit of dependence to add coverage."

"What about the baby's last name? Can it have Matt's, if that's what we want?"

"Yes. The baby can have either our last name or Matt's. The decision is entirely up to you."

On Wednesday, after school, Monica and I are driving around in her car. We have the stereo turned down low so we can talk. We're discussing the accident again. There was yet another major article about it in the paper, but this time it had a lot of personal stuff about the two girls who died. They were both sixteen-year-old juniors at North View High. Tory, as it turns out, was in a band with her friend Jenna. They both played the guitar and sang. Tory's mom described her as a "free spirit," and a friend of Jenna said she was "a musician at heart."

We're heading toward downtown Lakeview when Monica suddenly makes a sharp right, turning onto Lakeview Avenue. "I want to drive by there," she says. There's no missing the place where the accident happened.

Six or seven people are standing beside the light pole. One girl is crying. Balloons and flowers and notes for Tory and Jenna are scattered everywhere. Monica parks the car, and we walk over to the light pole. We just stand there, reading the notes.

"*Sing Forever Jenna.*"

"*To Tory, a revolutionary, kick-ass, beautiful person. You will be missed.*"

"*To Tory and Jenna: We'll miss you always!*"

"You know what I keep thinking, Ali?" Monica says when we get back to the car.

"What?"

"It could have been me. It could have been me."

Niles isn't in school all week. Everyone's still talking about the accident, even the teachers. In some ways, everything's the same. Here I am, going to class, taking notes, eating lunch, as I always do. I even remember to see my guidance counselor about getting out of P.E. next semester. She suggests taking a photography class because I'm planning to study journalism in college. "Sure," I say. Anything has to be better than P.E.

But in some ways, everything's different. Between classes, people don't seem to be laughing as much or messing around in the halls the way they usually do. There's just a low hum of voices. I write about it in my journal in English class, and as I read it over, I realize that maybe there's a germ of an idea in it for a column, so I rip it out and stuff it in my pocket.

Then on Friday, the last day before winter break, Monica gives me a lift home. It's been snowing all afternoon, and the roads are slick, so Monica drives slower than usual. We see Niles Sherman, walking along the road in the opposite direction.

Monica notices him first. He's hunched over, wearing a brown coat that hangs to his knees, but it's hanging open so you can see his arm in a blue sling. Monica honks the horn to get his attention, then makes a U-turn at the light, so we can give him a lift to wherever he's headed.

But by the time she turns the car around, he's already gone.

Chapter 16

On Christmas day, I wear one of the dressier maternity outfits Aunt Laura bought for me when I was in Chicago. It feels strange, like I'm wearing clothes that belong to someone else.

"You look darling," Mom says when I come downstairs. I have on the black slacks with a matching top. "Dad's on the phone with Grandma Jeanne. She wants to say hello to you."

I go into the den. Dad told Grandma last week, but I don't want to talk with her at all. I'm afraid she's going to start off by saying something like, "So you had SEX!?" Then she'll follow it up with a lecture about how disappointed she is in me. But it isn't like that at all.

"I am so sorry . . ." Grandma says, her voice breaking. "So sorry . . . this is happening to you." I hear her blow her nose. "I love you, Allison, and I believe in you. We Parker women are strong. You *will* get through this."

An hour later, Aunt Laura arrives to spend the day with us. We exchange presents. Mom and Dad give me two maternity tops, a book, a pair of earrings I've been wanting, and a 35 mm camera for my photography class next semester. "Now you can express yourself without words," says my mother. She's more excited about this class than I am.

Aunt Laura gives me denim maternity shorts. "I thought you might need them this spring," she says. I'm more excited about the shorts.

We have brunch afterwards, and Aunt Laura fills us in on her love life. "I've met someone new," she confides. "He might be the one."

Then my dad says something about managed care and a new drug they're coming out with, and I just listen to them talk about nothing and nothing and nothing. All I can think about is Matt. He's planning to stop by later, but he said he'd call first. We've only seen each other twice since school let out for winter break. I've been working almost every day from eleven to four, and he's been working nights at Vincent's and hanging out a lot with Niles.

Finally, he calls at 4:00, and when he comes by, my parents and Aunt Laura are in the family room working on a puzzle.

"Can we go somewhere to talk?" he says.

"Sure," I say, leading him to the den. It's the first room off the entryway of our home and very private. I sit on the sofa, opposite Matt.

"Here," he says, reaching into his coat pocket. He hands me a tiny box, wrapped in silver paper with blue ribbon. As soon as I see it, my heart nearly stops. Inside is a thick silver band. It doesn't look anything like an engagement ring, but then Matt takes it from the box and slips it on the ring finger of my left hand, and it looks just right.

"I'm thinking we could, uh, get married. I'll get a job, put off college for a year, maybe two, and save money. Maybe I can get a construction job again, or something else that pays well. We'll find a way to make this work."

I can't talk. The tears start coming. He kisses one cheek, then the other.

"I love you, Allison Parker," he says. Then he takes my hand to examine the ring. It's a little loose, but I like the way it looks on my hand. "The guy at the store said you could come in so they can size it."

"Wow," I say. "It's so beautiful."

Then the baby moves, so I take Matt's hand and put it on my stomach. "Can you feel it?" I ask him, covering his hand with mine. He can't at first, but then there's an undeniable ripple.

"That's amazing," he says, smiling.

"What do you think of the name Willow for the baby?" I ask.

"Willow . . . like a *tree?*"

I smile. "Yeah, like a tree."

"For a boy?" Matt looks skeptical.

"No, a girl. I found it in a book, and I think it's a pretty name."

Matt pretends like he's going to puke. "Oh yeah, sure, and if it's a boy we can name him after a planet, like Jupiter or Mars."

I give him a friendly poke. "I'm being serious here."

"So am I."

"Okay, then. What about Shana for a girl, and Jordan for a boy?"

He considers them both for a minute. "I like Shana, especially if she looks like you . . . but Jordan? Isn't that a girl's name?"

"It's unisex."

"No way," he says. "No unisex names."

"Okay . . ." I say, and try some of my other favorite names. "How about Justin?"

Matt shakes his head. "I once knew a kid named Justin. Couldn't stand him."

"Joshua?"

"Too pretty."

"Well, what names do you like?"

"You like J-names, right?"

I nod.

"Well, how about Jonah?"

"Jonah?" I don't usually like traditional names, but Jonah isn't one of those names you hear often, which almost makes it seem new.

"Yeah, I went to school with a guy named Jonah back in Ohio. He was cool. Everyone liked him."

I try it out. "Jonah Matthew Ryan."

"Do you like it?"

"It's growing on me."

"Do we *have* to use my name?"

"I love your name."

"Okay, okay," he says, as if he doesn't want to bother arguing with me, but I can tell he likes the idea of using his name.

Then he pulls me close and gives me a quick kiss, and I give him his presents—a CD he's been wanting and a blue sweater I knew would look good with his eyes. He puts it on right away. "Thanks," he says. Then we sit there on the sofa, holding hands and talking the way we used to, but an hour later, he has to leave. All his relatives are coming for dinner, and his parents expect him to be there.

The rest of the day, all I can think about is that Matt and I are getting married. I can't believe it's happening. *Mrs. Matthew Gregory Ryan. Allison Parker Ryan.* I write it out on a scratch pad and doodle all around it, making hearts and crescent moons and stars, but then I tear it up so no one will see it, especially my parents.

See, if I was living in 1952, I'd tell my parents right away, and they would probably weep with relief. But this is the 21st century. I doubt they'll think getting married is the answer to my situation. My parents have been steering me towards college since the day I was born. And now, whether I have a baby or not, they still want me to get a college degree. So I keep the news to myself and the ring out of sight. I need to think about how I'm going to tell them.

I tell myself that everything is starting to fall into place, but I get nervous and jumpy inside whenever I think of the future. I know it won't be easy. I mean, I haven't even graduated from high school yet, and now there's college to think about, and the baby. But it's Christmas, the lights on the tree are bright, and I have this ring that proves Matt's serious about this. Of course, another part of me just can't imagine it. I just can't.

It's two days after Christmas. We have another week off before school starts, and I'm in the kitchen making spaghetti sauce for dinner because my mom has to work late. The phone rings. As soon as I answer it, Matt says, "Guess where we're going next Friday?" He sounds excited. I haven't heard him like this in a long time.

I shift the phone to my other ear and play along, but after three guesses, I give up. "Where?"

"Skiing."

"I can't ski."

"Sure you can. I'll teach you."

"Matt, I know *how* to ski, but I can't. I'm pregnant. Remember?"

"Oh, right. I thought you're not *that* pregnant yet so it would be okay. It's just that some other people from work are going to a place in Wisconsin, and they asked if we want to come along." He sounds disappointed.

"I can't. I'm almost five months pregnant." He doesn't say anything. "Just because I can't go doesn't mean you can't."

"Are you sure?"

"Yeah."

"Great."

I hang up and wonder why it bothers me so much that he's going without me.

I still can't stop thinking about Niles and Tory and how everything can change so fast. And sometimes I wonder what would have happened if they took a different road that night or started out five minutes later. Would Tory and Jenna still be alive? One afternoon, I pull out the paper I wrote in English about the accident and try to write a column, which is due the day we get back to school. I have about two pages, double-spaced, but they're only words on paper. I'm not sure what I'm trying to say. I crumple it up and toss it in the garbage.

❧

"Things are getting serious with Kyle," Monica announces on New Year's Day. We're at my house making brownies, listening to music, and dancing around the kitchen in our bare feet. My parents went to a movie, so we have the music turned up louder than usual.

Monica broke things off with College Boy a while ago, which makes Kyle number 18. I shoot her a skeptical look. I've never seen her serious about anyone. Then I notice the initials K.M. with a heart drawn around them on the inside of Monica's wrist. Now she's writing his initials on her arm? *Gak.* I've never seen her like this over any guy. I pretend not to notice.

"I mean it," she says. "Kyle might just be the one."

"Does your mom know?" I ask, scraping the batter into a dish.

"No. We've been careful. Kyle took me to a party last night, and Mom said she was so relieved Kyle and I are getting along better. Then, *get this*, she asked how I like having a brother." Monica laughs. "If she only knew . . ."

I slide the brownies into the oven and look at her. "Mon, are you sleeping with him?"

"No, but believe me, he's interested." She smiles, scrapes the last of the batter from the bowl, and licks it off the spoon.

I just stand there, looking at her. You'd think that when your best friend is pregnant, that would be a serious reality check, but it doesn't even faze her.

"Why are you looking at me like that?" she asks.

"Because . . ."

"Because why?"

"Because I know what you're doing. And I know you have this
. . . *timeline*, but there are serious consequences here . . ." I say
in my Mom voice.

"Look, it's not about a timeline, Ali—not anymore. I've never
felt this way before. I love him."

"Have you told him that?"

She pulls her hair back with one hand and looks away. "Not
yet."

"Does he love you?"

"Oh, Ali . . . yes," she says, but she doesn't look completely
sure.

"He told you."

"Not in so many words . . . but I can tell."

I shoot her a look.

"What?" she says.

I shake my head.

"Just say it," she says.

"Look, if you can't even *talk* about how you're feeling . . .
that should tell you something."

On the last Friday in January, I have an ultrasound. Matt was
planning to go with me because we agreed we wanted to know
the sex of the baby. But at the last minute, Matt's dad decides to
take him and his brother skiing for the weekend. *Skiing!* It's all
Matt seems to think about now, and he can't wait to go. His dad
is picking him up from school right before lunch. "You can tell me
later," Matt says, as if it's no big deal.

Mom goes with me instead. As soon as I see the baby on the
screen, I get all choked up. There it is, sucking its thumb. Mom
reaches over and squeezes my hand.

"It's really something to see, isn't it? Still gets me every time," says the technician. Then she asks whether I want to know if it's a boy or girl.

"Yes," I say, but the baby never gets in the right position so we can see. My mom tells me we'll have to wait to find out the sex of the baby until after its born because Dad's insurance pays for only one ultrasound, unless there are complications. I have to admit, I'm disappointed. But it doesn't really matter. I can wait until it's born. Besides, I want Matt to be with me when we find out.

That Sunday, I save the real estate section from the newspaper so I can call about an apartment for me and Matt. I still haven't told my parents about our plans. The ring is hidden in the bottom of my pajama drawer, where I put it Christmas day. I still don't think my parents can handle that right now. Besides, I want to make sure getting married is going to work. On Monday, during lunch at school, I start making phone calls.

But after a few calls, I don't see how it can work. A two-bedroom apartment in downtown Chicago will run at least $800 a month, and every place I call wants the first *and* last month's rent up front plus a security deposit. I was thinking that if Matt got accepted at SAIC, it would be easier to live in the city. But even if Matt worked two jobs and I got a job, we would never have enough money to cover all our expenses.

Then I call several apartment complexes in nearby suburbs, but even those are out of our price range. I think about what Ms. Connor said at our first meeting. "You may get help from your parents, your boyfriend, or your friends," she said, "but you need to find out what they are willing to provide."

That night, I finally tell my parents our plan. "I think getting married is a bad idea," Dad says, setting his glass of wine on the table next to the sofa. He and Mom were in the den talking when I sprang it on them.

"But it will solve everything," I say, crossing my arms.

"You're both very young," Mom says. "You'll ruin your lives

if you make a mistake. You've already made one mistake. Don't compound it with another."

"Look, I don't think you understand. This isn't just some high school romance, okay?" My eyes fill with tears. I don't want to cry, but I can't help it.

"Ali, you know we've always liked Matt," Dad begins. "But we don't want you to get married—not yet, not now, and not for the wrong reasons. I think the best thing for both you and Matt would be to continue your education."

"We will. We thought we would get married and take a year off after the baby comes—to save money and get a head start— then go to school the following year," I say. It makes perfect sense. They have to understand. "The only thing is, we'll need some money to help with expenses."

Dad looks at Mom and then at me. "Ali, we've been talking," he says carefully. "We think it would be best if you went to college in the fall as planned. We've already set money aside for tuition. We thought you could take evening classes at the university. That way, your mom and I are here to take care of the baby at night."

"But what's the difference whether I live here or live with Matt? I'm just asking if you could help us financially a little. You know, give us some of the money you planned on using for my tuition."

"Ali, we think getting married now, or even living together, is a big mistake," Mom says.

"You can't tell me what to do. I'll be eighteen in June."

Dad sighs. "We realize that, Ali."

"But we cannot support what we believe would be a bad choice," Mom says.

"I thought you guys were on my side," I say, knowing full well I sound childish.

"Ali," Dad says, "we *are* on your side."

Chapter 17

The photography class is in the vocational building next to the parking lot. The teacher is Mr. Guiterrez, but everyone calls him Mr. G. He doesn't look anything like the other teachers at Lakeview. He has long dark hair and a goatee, wears cargo pants, and uses the type of language you don't usually hear from teachers.

It turns out his photography class is insanely popular because he doesn't believe in giving homework or tests. But the first week is boring because he explains the parts of the camera and talks about light, focus, f-stops, and perspective. The second week doesn't get any better. We get an in-depth tour of the photo lab and demonstrations on how to develop film. I almost wish I was back in P.E., but then he turns us loose with our cameras and tells us to "get creative . . . find your muse."

The first opportunity we have to be creative is at Willow Lake. I use half a roll of film snapping various shots of the lake, which is frozen. I snap a few shots of the trees and the concession stand that has a black and orange sign that reads "Closed—See you this spring!" But I'm seriously uninspired—maybe because it's freezing outside, or maybe it's because I have no talent. I'm better with words. (Not that you'd know it lately.)

Later, when we're back at school, I still have a few pictures left. The bell hasn't rung yet, so the halls are empty. I pop the lens cap off my camera, snapping the hall in front of the principal's office by all the rows of lockers. It's usually jammed with people going to and from class, but no one's around now. It looks deserted and creepy. Then, turning a corner, I see someone off in the distance, alone, hunched over by a row of lockers, leaning his head against a locker. I snap the picture, catching him in that one instant with a click. He turns to leave, and as he walks away, I realize it's Niles.

The next day in the darkroom, when we develop our pictures, I stand and watch as Niles' image emerges slowly in the solution tray. Then, all of a sudden, there it is—a silhouette in black and white, perfect and haunting. When Mr. G. walks by, he stops and looks down for a long time. "Excellent contrast . . . a row of lockers, a lone figure off in the distance. It looks like you caught him off guard," he says in a voice only I can hear, his eyes still on the photo. "It's almost as if you can feel his pain."

When class is over, I grab a tuna sandwich in the cafeteria and head over to Ms. Connor's office. Kelly and I meet with Ms. Connor during lunch on Mondays and Wednesdays. Sometimes Ms. Connor talks with us about something specific like prenatal care and eating healthy. Other times, she lets Kelly and I ask questions or discuss whatever's on our minds. Today, I want to talk with Ms. Connor about my mother. Lately, avoiding her has become my other part-time job. Whenever Mom is alone with me, she starts in about how marrying Matt will ruin my life. I've heard this lecture now, oh, about two dozen times. And Matt is no help. He's mentioned marriage exactly *two times* since Christmas, and talked about how great it will be when we have our own place, but he's not doing anything to make it happen.

Kelly's already there. As soon as I walk in, she says, "Connor had to take off . . . something about her daughter and an ear infection." Then she screws the top off a Coke, takes a swig, and says, "Guess what happened to me yesterday?"

"What?"

"My parents kicked me out of the house."

"*Really?* Wow. . ." And I thought *my* parents were bad—especially my mother and her endless lectures. At least they didn't disown me or anything.

"Yeah."

"So where are you living?"

"With Jared."

"I'm sorry." I give her a sympathetic look.

"You know what? It's better—really. Once they found out I was pregnant, my stepfather didn't want me around, and my mother just doesn't want to be bothered. Besides, I have Jared and this little guy." She pats her belly. Kelly doesn't know for sure what she's having, but she thinks it'll be a boy. "I have my own family now."

"Have you told Ms. Connor?"

She polishes off her Coke and burps. "Yep. She knows."

"So what are you going to do after the baby comes?" Her baby is due in April, just two months away.

"God," she says, "you sound *just like* Ms. Connor. Maybe you should be a shrink. Jared thinks I should quit school, but Ms. Connor is really pushing me to graduate, and I don't want to let her down. And . . . I'm getting married." She smiles and flashes an engagement ring with a diamond so tiny it's practically nonexistent.

"That's great," I say, though I don't mean it. I met Jared when he picked Kelly up from school one day. I can't say exactly what it is about him that bothers me, but I just don't like him.

"After the baby comes, though, I'm going to get a job. I have to. Jared makes good money and everything, but the rent where we live is steep and we're going to have a lot of extra expenses once the baby's born."

Before I leave for my next class, Kelly says, "You want to come over and help me on Saturday? I bought a border that I want to put up. And I thought I'd paint some balloons or something on the walls."

We've never hung out together outside of Ms. Connor's office, so I'm a little surprised she wants to get together. "Sure," I say. "I'm working the early shift on Saturday, but I can come by in the afternoon." I like hanging out with her. Right now, Kelly is the only person on the planet who really knows how I'm feeling.

The next day, between classes, I show Monica my navel in the girls' restroom. No one else is around.

"Look at this," I say, turning to the side and pulling my shirt up so she can get a clear view. "It looks like a timer on a turkey."

"Oh, yeah," she says, "a protruding navel. You're lucky. That was supposed to happen last month."

"What am I going to do?"

"Oh, Ali, it hardly shows at all," she says, which is, of course, the correct answer, though we both know it's not true.

❧

Kelly and Jared live in an apartment on the edge of town. I've been wanting to see it all week. Kelly says it's a small garden apartment, and I keep thinking it's probably the sort of place Matt and I should get. But it's not like anything I pictured. It's tiny and dark and stinks from stale cigarettes and pot. The so-called "garden" consists of one rose bush and a patch of weeds outside the back door.

"This is it," Kelly says. You'd think it was a mansion, the way she shows me around.

There's a living room, a tiny kitchen, a bathroom, and two bedrooms.

"It's great," I say, nodding and smiling like an idiot. But the truth is, I can't imagine living here. It's depressing. There isn't much furniture—just an ugly green couch with a huge brown stain on it and an old rocker. But there are some posters of dolphins on the walls that make the place look a little cheerier.

"*And this* . . . is the nursery," says Kelly, leading me to the smaller of the two bedrooms. It's the best room in the place. It looks clean, for one thing, and there's a crib already set up in the corner.

"It smells like you just painted the room."

"Jared did it yesterday. He wasn't real thrilled about doing it, but I can't—you know, the fumes and all. And I want the baby's room to be nice."

"Where did you get the crib?"

"At a garage sale. It was $30. New ones cost as much as $400, and that doesn't even include the mattress!"

"Wow. I had no idea."

By late afternoon, Kelly and I have hung the border, and Kelly is painting a huge apple tree in one corner, along with some clouds and a red kite. The bedroom window is open to let in fresh air.

"I didn't know you could paint like that," I say, admiring Kelly's handiwork.

"Thanks."

"You should go to art school."

"Four more years? No thanks. I hate school."

Just then the door slams. "Jar, is that you?" Kelly calls.

"Yeah."

"Come here. I want to show you the nursery."

He ambles in and looks around. Right away, I can tell he's stoned. He smells like weed, and his eyes are red. "Looks great," he says, but it sounds like he couldn't care less.

"Remember Ali?" Kelly asks.

"Uh . . ." he says, laughing. "Not really." He sounds goofy.

Jared walks back into the living room, and Kelly asks if I want something to drink. "Sure," I say. Jared sits down on the sofa, pulls a baggy from his pocket, and starts rolling a joint. "Want some?" he offers.

"No thanks," I say, and he looks up and smiles, as if he's relieved. I tried pot a few times freshman year, but it just made me depressed. And once I was so hungry afterward that I ate an entire can of ravioli without even bothering to heat it up. Who needs help getting depressed and hungry? To be honest, I don't see the point.

Kelly pours both of us orange juice in two plastic cups. We talk for a while and then head back to the baby's room to admire the walls.

"Why don't we do something next week?" I say just before I leave.

"Sure," Kelly says.

I hate to admit it, but the truth is, I probably would never have anything to do with someone like Kelly if she wasn't pregnant. But now, we have a lot in common.

❦

That night, Matt and I go out for pizza. In between bites, he says, "I called Al, the guy who helped me get the construction job last summer. He said it shouldn't be a problem getting me a full-time job after graduation. The pay is great, and that way we can save a lot of money." Matt reaches for another slice. "So, I figure maybe we can both sit out a year or so. Maybe you can get a job, too, and we can both start college the following year. You think your parents will still pay for school?"

His plan sounds good, but I don't know if it'll work. Lately, I've become more aware of the cost of things. Last week, Ms. Connor had me check out the costs of diapers, formula, and clothes, and then look at how much Matt and I would be earning every month. Kelly told me that Jared has a good job with the city, but now that I've seen their apartment, the last thing I want is to be in the same situation as Kelly and Jared.

❦

It turns out that AP English has a sequel—AP English II. The class roster is identical to last semester's, minus a few people who couldn't take another semester of Carrot Top. "We can hardly consider the human experience without first thinking of Hamlet," says Carrot Top, waving her sacred book like a TV evangelist.

Monica sits next to me, just like last semester, and we're still slogging through *Hamlet*, which Monica and I complain about daily. Any *normal* teacher would be able to get through one play in a semester, but Carrot Top is about as far from normal as you can get. Monica tries out new nicknames for Carrot Top in class: Red-Headed Freak . . . Shakespeare Nazi . . . Hamlet Harpy.

Niles is still there, in the back row, but he's not the same as he was last semester. He doesn't bring in outrageous words like "concupiscence" or find ingenious ways to push Carrot Top's buttons. He just sits there in class, staring straight ahead, eyes glazed over, as if he sees nothing.

At the start of March, I'm seven months pregnant and as big as a whale. As it turns out, I don't actually have to tell anyone I'm pregnant because it's obvious. Everyone at school is talking about me. Monica says I'm paranoid, but she's just being nice. I see the way people look at me—the way everyone stares. I was walking down the hall one day with Matt when a group of girls passed by us, whispering and looking my way.

Then, the other afternoon, I walked into the bathroom. Everyone was talking, there was a fog of cigarette smoke and perfume, and the hiss of hairspray. As soon as I walked in, everyone stopped talking and stared at me, just for a split second, but I know I didn't imagine it.

The only person I actually *tell* about my pregnancy is Andy. We were working on an article one day about how to ace the SAT, and he kept staring at my waist. So I just told him. Andy's cheeks turned bright pink, and his ears turned even pinker, if that's possible. He acted strange for a while, but then he seemed to forget about it, and now we're okay. We insult each other and joke around, and everything's back to normal, except that occasionally he'll ask me how it's going or what it's like. And when we work on articles together, he brings me granola bars from the snack machine instead of candy. As for everyone else, I don't care any more. After graduation, I won't be seeing everyone at school.

***

At the end of the month, I get a rejection letter from Columbia and acceptance letters from Northwestern and NYU.

"That's great, Ali," Monica says when I show her the acceptance letters. We're at Monica's house. Monica is sitting on the floor of her room carefully painting her toenails Miami Beach Blue. She has a cotton ball between each toe. Monica was accepted at the University of Illinois but is still waiting to hear from Northwestern.

"Oh, sure," I say. "I can take the baby with me to classes."

"You're so . . . *irritable*," she says. It's a word I know she picked up from the prenatal book.

"I am not."

"Okay, if you say so . . ." she says, raising her eyebrows, and turning her attention back to her toes. "I thought your mom and dad offered to help."

"Yeah, well . . ." I shake my head. "They have, but I'm not exactly sure how that's going to play out. My mom works nine to five, and my dad's schedule is even worse. There's no way I can go to school full time."

"Ali, you're not really going to get married, are you?" Monica thinks I'm crazy to even consider it.

"I thought you liked Matt."

"I do, but you have too much going for you to get married and play mommy."

"What's wrong with being a mother?" I pick up my camera

and start clicking. Monica's toes might make an interesting shot. The nail polish still looks wet.

"Nothing, but you can't be Ali-Parker-The-Teenager-Who-Got-Pregnant for the rest of your life. You know what I mean?"

I know she's right, but I just say, "You're a pain in the ass. You know that, right?"

She turns to me and sticks out her tongue. *Click.* Got it. "Yeah, well, that's what best friends are for."

Then I ask her about Kyle.

"I think we'll do something drastic soon."

I give her a look.

"Mom and Steve are going on a cruise during spring break, so we'll have the house to ourselves for a week. We're going to wait until then."

I put the camera down. "Mon, are you *ready?* I mean, do you feel *really ready?*"

She looks at me and gets quiet, the way she does when she's irritated, but I don't care. "Why are you doing this?" she asks.

"I just want you to be really sure." My hand drops to my stomach. I feel a familiar ripple and kick, as if the baby's underscoring my point. "Look, I thought I was ready. I mean, I knew I loved Matt, and I felt so ready, but now, it's really hard. We never *imagined* that something like this could happen. But I loved him and it seemed right at the time . . ."

"That's just it, Ali. I love him, he loves me, and you know what? He's older. It's not like we can sit around holding hands and kissing forever."

"Don't sleep with him just to hold onto him."

"It's not like that."

I know I should let it go, but I can't. "Once you sleep with him, it'll change everything," I say. "And if you break up or if you get pregnant . . . you need to think about that."

On Thursday, which is Matt's birthday, he shows Monica and me two letters at lunch. One is from SAIC, and the other is from

Pratt. He's been accepted at both places.

"Matt, that's great," I say, but really I just want to fall apart.

"Hey, you're on your way!" Monica says, which is the worst thing she could say.

"Yeah. On my way to nowhere," he says.

"What's that supposed to mean?" I ask.

"Nothing. Forget it." He picks up his lunch tray. "I have a trig test to study for. Catch you later."

On his way out, a girl with shiny dark hair, who is irritatingly pretty, touches his arm. I can't hear what they're saying, but he smiles at her and says something that makes her toss her hair to one side and laugh. Then he falls into step beside her, and they leave the cafeteria together.

"Who's that?" I ask Monica.

"Lauren Thompson. She just moved here from Texas."

I don't say a word. I'm not the jealous type, but there's something about the way Matt looked at Lauren. I know that look.

I have a dream that night about the baby. Matt and I are living in Kelly and Jared's apartment and taking care of the baby. I'm in college, but I can't make it to my classes on time, no matter how hard I try. The baby is constantly crying, and won't stop. Matt is yelling that it's all my fault, and then Lauren Thompson is holding the baby until it stops. Then I wake up.

A week before spring break, Matt calls me. "I don't know how to tell you this, but my parents are going to Florida for spring break, and they want me to go. They're renting an RV and want to camp along the coast. They think I need to get away."

"So go."

"You don't mind?"

"No."

"What about the baby?"

"The baby's not due till the end of May."

"I can tell you're pissed."

The truth is, I am. Why shouldn't I be? My parents always plan a trip over spring break, but we can't go anywhere this year because of the baby. Plus, everyone's planning for prom. It doesn't matter that I've never really been into the prom thing or that I don't want to go because I'll be nine months pregnant. I always thought I would boycott it actually. The prom itself is pretty much like being in the cafeteria at lunchtime. Still, Matt could at least ask if I *want* to go. *He hasn't even asked!*

"I'm not," I say, pretending that it doesn't matter. "Look, just go and have a good time. Okay?"

"All right. You'll call me, though, right? If anything, uh, comes up?"

"Sure."

"Great," he says. "Well, see ya."

"Oh, Matt, what about—"

Click. It's too late. He's gone. I was about to tell him about the childbirth classes I signed up for on Wednesday nights at the hospital. Classes start next week, and I was hoping he'd go with me when he doesn't have to work.

Chapter 18

Maybe I'm a glutton for punishment, but I watch The Weather Channel every day during spring break. It's sunny and hot in Florida and wet and cold in Chicago. Matt calls twice to see how I am, but our conversations are short and to the point. His last call went like this.

"Hi, it's me," he said. "How are you?"

"Fine." He doesn't even ask about the baby. There was a long and uncomfortable pause.

"How's the weather?" I asked.

"Great."

I heard voices and laughter in the background. "Are you having fun?" I asked.

"I'm sorry," he said. I can tell he's laughing at something someone said, and I swear I heard a girl say his name. "What?"

"Forget it."

"Want me to call again in a day or so?" he asked.

Not if you have to ask, I wanted to say. But instead I said, "No, I'm fine."

⌇

St. Mary's Hospital conducts free health screenings every spring for senior citizens at the mall. The hospital's Community Relations Department coordinates the event, and Mom insists I help out because she thinks it'll be good for me to do something "constructive." I don't want to at first. I don't want the people

Mom works with to see me pregnant. "Look, it'll be fine," Mom assures me on the drive over. "They already know . . . And besides, we really need your help for the next two days. We're short on volunteers."

It isn't too bad. On the first day, Mom's boss, Abby, hugs me and says she thinks of me a lot. And JC, who's the editor of their publications, tells me her neighbor's daughter got pregnant at sixteen. "I'm not saying it's easy," JC says, "but it's not the end of the world."

The second day, I pass out gift bags from the hospital and direct people to the screening booths. About halfway through the day, I notice a bluish mark above my left knee but don't think much of it. It's probably from the marker I used to make a poster for one of the booths.

But later that night, when it doesn't wash off in the shower, I worry and show it to my mom. "What is it?"

Mom, stooping down to get a closer look, rubs a finger over it. "I think it's a varicose vein."

A varicose vein! I'm too young to have a varicose vein! "I thought that just happened to old people."

"Sometimes it happens during pregnancy," Mom says matter-of-factly, as if it's no big deal.

"Will it go away after the baby comes?"

"Mmm . . . probably not. But when you get some sun this summer, it won't show as much."

I spend the rest of spring break working at Java House and taking photographs of people. In photography class, we're done with landscapes and objects, and now we're working on people for our final project. I like shooting pictures of people the best, but not formal portraits, which always look stiff. I like to catch people off guard. I found my dad the other afternoon on the back porch, talking to the neighbor's golden retriever. My dad was crouched down, talking with the dog, their noses touching. Then this morning, I saw my mom standing in the kitchen, looking out the window at nothing. I picked up the camera, popped off the cap, and said "Mom . . ." She turned toward me, looking startled. *Click.* She wasn't smiling.

On Wednesday, I go to my first childbirth class. Mom goes with me because Matt is in Florida. The nurse shows the class a life-size model of a pelvis and points to the opening where the baby will come out. When I see it, all I can think is that she must be joking. How can a baby make it through an opening *that* small?

On Thursday, I'm working at Java House when Monica stops by to pick up her paycheck. I was about to go on break, so we go outside to talk, but not before I get a decaf cappuccino, and Monica goes for the high octane. I'm wearing my green Java House apron. Monica is wearing low-slung jeans, chunky platform boots, and a sweater with the American flag on the front. She's been dressing a little less flamboyantly since things heated up with Kyle.

"I'm no longer a virgin," Monica dramatically announces as soon as we sit down at an outdoor table.

"When?" Her news doesn't surprise me that much. The way she's been talking recently, I realized it was just a matter of time.

"Last night. Mom and Steve are on their cruise."

"Do they know he's staying over?"

"Are you crazy? He told them he was working over spring break.

They think he's at school."

"I hope you know what you're doing, Mon."

"I've never felt like this with any other guy. I'm in love."

I stir my cappuccino and try not to smile. The L-word sounds funny coming from someone like Monica. She used to think that sex and love not only can be separated, but should be.

"So, aren't you going to ask me how it was?"

"I thought you might want to keep that part private."

"You are so proper . . . for someone who's knocked up," she says gamely, licking the froth from a stirrer. We share the laugh, but then Monica gets serious. "It's quite possibly the most intense experience of my life. And I'm so relieved I'll never have to go through this first-time business again. But I can't help feeling a little let down. I mean, everyone makes such a big deal out of it. I didn't come, but I felt so close to him that it didn't matter. He's very hung up on me coming. Have you ever had an orgasm?"

"Nope."

"You're kidding? Not once? After all this time?"

I shake my head. "Aunt Laura says that's normal. According to her, it takes a lot of practice. She didn't have one until she was twentysomething."

"Hmm. In the movies, everyone is always having orgasms." Monica sighs. "I just wanted it to be perfect."

"Where *is* Kyle, anyway?"

"He went back to the dorm to pick up his stuff. He's spending the weekend with me."

Just then her cell phone rings. She picks it up on the first ring, smiles, and lowers her voice. I pick at my cup and pretend not to listen. Then she says, "I love you. No, I love you more. I do," she says, twirling a lock of hair around and around her finger.

When she hangs up, I just shake my head. "You are *so* pathetic," I say, but the truth is, I'm a little jealous. It seems like forever since I felt that way.

<hr>

The phone rings that night at 10:30. I'm in bed, but I haven't fallen asleep yet. I pick up the phone on the first ring, hoping it's Matt, but it's not.

"Sorry to call so late, but I wanted you to know . . . I had my baby," says Kelly. Her voice is so hoarse I almost don't recognize it.

"Wow, congratulations!" I try to sound excited for her, but the truth is, I'd rather be talking to Matt. "When was it born?"

"This afternoon, at 1:08. It's a girl. We named her Erica. She weighs six pounds, three ounces." She sounds euphoric.

"But it's only the first week of April." Her baby wasn't due until the end of the month.

"Yeah. It's a good thing the nursery is ready."

Before we hang up, I promise to stop by and see her the next day.

"Okay," Kelly says. "But come by the apartment. We're checking out of the hospital at noon."

The next morning, when I tell my parents the news about Kelly, Mom asks if she can come along. Kelly and my mom met a few weeks ago when I invited her to dinner, and they hit it off right away. Mom spends the morning making her famous veggie lasagna to take with us.

Later that afternoon, on the way to Kelly and Jared's apartment, Mom pulls into a drug store to pick up perfume for Kelly, along with a jumbo-sized bag of diapers for newborns. "I just want to get her something," she says. "Sometimes, new moms need a pick-me-up," she explains, peeling the price tag off the perfume and dropping it into a gift bag.

It's a good perfume, the kind they keep locked in a glass case. I had gone out earlier to buy the baby a tiny pair of shorts and a t-shirt with a dog on the front. With tax, they cost more than twenty-five dollars. I couldn't believe it.

When we get there, Jared opens the door, eyes red, reeking of pot. "Hey," he says, waving us in. I don't think I've ever seen him when he wasn't stoned. "I'm on my way out," he says, grabbing his jacket off the sofa and moving his bong off the coffee table, but not before my mom sees it. She glances away and says something about the weather.

Before he leaves, he hands Kelly a bottle for the baby, then leans down and kisses the top of Erica's head, which makes me like him more—not much more, though.

"I hope you don't mind my tagging along," Mom says, sitting

on the sofa next to Kelly.

"Oh, no," Kelly says, smiling. I wonder whether Kelly's own mother has even seen the baby yet.

"Oh, my. She *is* beautiful," says Mom, smoothing the baby's hair.

"Do you want to hold her?" Kelly asks.

"May I?" Mom reaches for her, then settles back on the couch and takes the bottle Kelly hands her.

I've been very cool to my parents since the whole marriage thing came up. But watching Mom talk to Kelly and feed the baby, I realize just how much she cares, and how great she's really handling everything.

Kelly looks tired but happy. I give her the presents, and Kelly seems especially touched by the perfume.

"So how was it?" I finally ask. "Tell me everything." I'm a little afraid of going through labor, and I spend a lot more time thinking about it now that I'm so close.

"Twenty-six hours of labor, three-and-a-half hours of pushing. I was so hungry, but they wouldn't let me eat anything except ice chips. Afterwards, Jar ordered me a pizza." She laughs.

"What a good eater she is," Mom says, holding up the empty bottle. She burps Erica on her shoulder. "Ali, do you want to hold her?"

I know I should, but I've never held a baby this small. Mom hands Erica to me, and I feel so awkward at first, I actually break out in a sweat. She's so tiny. But then Erica snuggles into the crook of my arm and falls asleep. She smells delicious, fresh and sweet, like baby powder.

That's when it hits me. Next month, I'll be responsible for a tiny little person just like the one I'm holding in my arms. No, that's not entirely right. *Matt and I will be responsible.* Just thinking of it scares me. We don't know *anything* about babies.

"Maybe we should start getting some things together for the baby," I tell Mom on the way home.

Mom keeps her eyes on the road. "Does that mean you and Matt have made definite plans?" she asks in that careful tone she seems to use so often with me lately.

"Not exactly."

"What does that mean?"

"We haven't worked out all the details, but as soon as Matt gets back from Florida . . ."

Mom sighs. "Ali, this isn't like playing house. This baby is for real."

"I know that." The last thing I need is another lecture. *Didn't I just say we should get some things together for the baby?*

"Ali, how do you and Matt plan to pay for all the things you'll need for a baby?"

"We have money." I have $1,200 in a savings account, and Matt has some money saved, too.

"Ali . . ."

"Please don't start." I can't handle another one of these discussions.

"Look, it's not like we're being irresponsible, okay? We're trying to work it all out."

"Oh, *really?*" Mom asks. "Then why is Matt in Florida?"

That gets me. "What does that have to do with anything?"

Mom doesn't say anything, but when she stops the car at a light, she turns to me. She looks likes she's about to cry. "I feel like I'm watching you jump off a cliff, and there's nothing I can do to save you."

Chapter 19

The next day, I walk over to Monica's house. Julie and Steve aren't coming back from their trip until tomorrow, but Kyle's already left to go back to school. Otherwise, I wouldn't go over. But when I ring the bell, Julie answers the door in one of her yoga outfits. "Monica's in her room," she says. She doesn't smile. Her mouth is a thin stiff line. She looks like a completely different person.

Monica is lying on her bed, listening to her stereo. Her eyes are red and puffy, the way they always get when she's been crying.

"What's going on?" I ask.

"They came home *early*. Mom and Steve saw us kissing in the hallway, and they came unglued. Mom's been lecturing me, and Kyle said his dad blew up."

"She's probably worried you'll end up like me."

Monica glances at me and looks away. "No," she says, shaking her head, but I know I guessed right. "Get this: she asked me if we were sleeping together or just *thinking* about it."

"What did you say?"

"*Are you kidding?* I didn't tell her anything. If she thought I was sexually active, she would have a nuclear meltdown."

There's a party that night at Greg Bartel's house. His parents are out of town, and he invited a group of kids over to hang out.

Monica and Greg are in the same criminal law class together, and Monica calls to see if I want to go. She can't stand being in her house another minute.

"No, thanks. I'm too tired," I say. But the truth is, I don't want to go. It's hard to blend in when you're almost eight months pregnant. I know everyone's talking about me. I haven't missed the long looks or the way everyone stops talking when I enter a room. There's no way I'm going to put myself through that.

Monica comes over the next morning after church. My parents and I had just gotten back ourselves, and we're sitting around the kitchen table, eating cinnamon rolls we picked up at a bakery. Monica is quiet, but I figure it's because her parents found out about her and Kyle.

Later, my parents leave to go grocery shopping. "How's it going?" I ask as soon as they're out the door.

"You have no idea. I called Kyle last night from Greg's house. We've decided to cool it for a while—at least around our parents."

I help myself to another cinnamon roll and take a bite. Their strategy makes sense to me. And who knows? Maybe he is the one, the boyfriend she will actually like for more than a few weeks. After all, she's declared undying love for this guy, and she's never done that before.

"Have you heard from Matt?" Monica says.

"He's not back yet." I get up to pour us each a glass of milk.

"Ali, if I know something . . . something that would hurt you . . . would you still want to know?"

Something in her voice makes me stop. I know Monica too well. This is definitely not a hypothetical question. I just look at her. "What?"

"Matt was at Greg's party last night."

"Oh." I flash freeze, and go numb, another layer of ice forming.

Monica looks at me carefully. "That Lauren person was there, too," she says.

"What are you trying to say?"

"She was hanging all over him."

"Did he see you?"

"Not at first. When I left, I asked him if you knew he was back in town. But I don't think he heard me. He was pretty drunk."

I leave both glasses of milk on the counter and sit down.

Monica looks at me worriedly. "Did I do the right thing? I couldn't sleep all night thinking about it."

I try to smile, but it's a lame effort. Sometimes the truth hurts. It really does. When Monica leaves, I call Matt, but no one answers, so I leave a message on the machine. He calls back later that afternoon.

"Hey, I'm back," he announces when I answer the phone.

"I heard," I say. A third layer of ice forms. I am Ice Queen.

He doesn't notice. "We got in last night, but it was too late to call, and I had to work this morning. This is the first chance I had to call."

He just flat-out lies to me, and it comes out so smoothly I can't believe it. "You don't have to explain anything to me, Matt."

"What's up with you?"

"Monica saw you last night. That's what's up."

"It's not what you think, Ali. Monica—"

Click. I hang up. I don't want to hear his lame excuses.

I see Matt at school on Monday during second period study hall. He's wearing a Mexican Baja pullover I've never seen before. It's cream with blue stripes and makes him look very tan. I wish he didn't look so good. I walk into class right when the bell rings, so there's no time to talk. I can feel him watching me, but I ignore him, pretending I couldn't care less if I ever talked to him again.

I try reading *Hamlet*, at the same time keeping a close eye on Matt while he chews on his pencil and struggles with trig. "Why e'en so, and now my Lady Worm's . . . knocked about the [mazard] with a sexton's spade." I read the same line over and over, fixating on "mazard," wondering why Matt doesn't slip me a note or try to get my attention. When the bell finally rings, I practically run down the hallway, but Matt catches up with me.

"Ali, wait," he says.

I know I shouldn't, but I do. Sometimes I'm an idiot.

"Look," he says, "it's not what you—"

"*Matt!* I'm *soooo* glad I ran into you," says Lauren, touching his arm. "I need to borrow your trig notes. Do you mind?" She smiles, sweeps her hair to one side, and tilts her head sweetly to look at him.

She's wearing low-slung jeans and a tight white t-shirt with a sunflower to show off her fake tan. Her waist is so tiny. I can't remember my waist ever being that tiny.

"Uh . . . sure," he says, glancing at me, then opening his backpack to look for the notes.

"I've got to get to class," I say.

Lauren looks at me as if seeing me for the first time, and as if I'm as insignificant to her as a blade of grass. Matt doesn't bother to introduce us. I walk away, wondering if Lauren knows I'm pregnant with his baby.

I avoid Matt at lunchtime. I feel fat, sick, and ready to explode. I don't want to see him, let alone talk with him. But after school, there he is, leaning against my mom's car in the parking lot, waiting for me.

"Do you mind?" I ask. He's standing in front of the driver's door.

"Can we talk?"

"What's there to talk about?"

"C'mon, Ali. You're so mad you can't see straight, and you haven't even heard my side of the story."

I don't want to fight. I really want to believe that it's all just some misunderstanding. "Okay. Get in."

He climbs into the passenger side of the car, and I drive to a nearby park.

"I want to know what happened Saturday night."

"Look, nothing happened," he says. "She—"

"Lauren?"

"Yeah, Lauren. She was pretty drunk, and she was just talking to me."

"Monica says she was hanging all over you and that you were drunk, too."

"Okay, yes, we were both drinking, but she's lonely, Ali. She just moved here, and she doesn't have many friends. And . . . I told her I had a girlfriend."

"Does she know it's *me?*" I'm starting to yell, but I can't help it.

"We didn't get that far. *Chill out* . . . There's no need to get hysterical."

"I am not hysterical! I just want to know what's going on!"

He shakes his head and sort of laughs. "Yeah, right," he says.

I take a deep breath and try to calm down. "So you were drunk?"

"Yeah."

"Did you sleep with her?" The thought of them together tears at me, but I have to know.

"No, nothing like that." He gives me a look and turns away. "Look, I may as well tell you. She kissed me. That's when I told her I have a girlfriend."

I don't want to hear any more. I start the car and pull out of the parking lot too fast.

"I never took you for the jealous type," he says.

"I'm not jealous. But stop pretending that nothing's going on. I'm not stupid."

"Look, Ali," he says. "It's just that . . . I got a little crazy Saturday night. I mean, with the baby . . . it's all kind of overwhelming sometimes, you know? It's a lot of responsibility."

"You're such an asshole! This is not exactly nirvana for me, either. I'm eight months pregnant, I barely fit behind the desks at school, and now you're playing these games!"

He snorts and shakes his head. "I'm here, aren't I? Any other guy would walk away."

We're back at the school parking lot. I have no problem finding his car—Lauren is standing next to it. A layer of ice twists around my heart, but I'm not about to let it show. "Oh, there's your *girlfriend*," I say nonchalantly. I stop the car hard. Matt steps out and slams the door shut. I take off so fast he has to jump back so I don't flatten his foot with my tire.

Chapter 20

I stop by Kelly's apartment after school the next day to take her some books. The school district is arranging for a tutor to help her, and Ms. Connor asked if I could drop off her books. Matt and I aren't speaking to one another. I'm trying to keep busy so I won't have time to think about my so-called life, which is a mess.

It's 4:00 when I get there, but Kelly looks as if she hasn't taken a shower yet. She's wearing sweatpants, a baggy t-shirt, and glasses. I've never seen her in glasses.

"Are you okay?" I ask, sitting next to her on the sofa. Erica is asleep in her infant seat.

"Just tired. Erica was crying on and off all night. I only slept for three hours."

"Does Jared help?"

"He tried at first, but it seems like she cries even harder when he holds her." Kelly sighs. "It's okay. He has to get up early for work every morning."

"Do you have anyone else who can help you?"

"My mom stopped by over the weekend. So at least she hasn't completely disowned me, but she works . . . and my stepfather still wants nothing to do with me or the baby."

"How about if I come over and babysit Saturday afternoon so you can go out? Besides, I need the practice."

"Sure. If you don't mind, that would be great." She smiles for the first time since I got there.

"Kelly, can I ask you something personal?"

"Sure."

"Did you and Jared fight a lot? I mean, before you had Erica?"

She rolls her eyes. "Oh, yeah, especially when I first told him. But then it was like we were the perfect couple, and we could picture everything—our own place, decorating the nursery, that sort of thing."

I look around the shabby apartment. "Is it what you thought it would be like?"

Kelly laughs. "Not even a little. I love Erica, and I really wanted someone of my own to love, but it's so hard. She needs attention 24/7 . . . She's like this love vacuum. Last night, I was exhausted . . . Erica was crying . . . we were trying to sleep, and Jared yells at me like it's my fault. There are times when I just sit here and cry because I'm not ready for it."

Later, right before I leave, Kelly says, "Since we're being honest, can I ask you something?"

"Sure."

"Did you get pregnant to hold onto Matt?"

"No. Why?"

"That's what I heard at school. Some of the girls are saying you got pregnant on purpose."

Matt and I are speaking again, but things aren't like they used to be. I see him less and less. His phone calls are shorter. And he's always working or going somewhere with Niles. So I ask Mom if she'll go to the childbirth class with me again on Wednesday night. The topic is labor and delivery, and I don't want to miss it. Mom doesn't ask why Matt isn't going.

The traffic is heavy that night, so we're ten minutes late. The room is dark when we walk in. Susan Fischer, the instructor, is standing next to her laptop. On the screen is a picture of a woman giving birth like a pro. "There are two seats in the corner," she says, waving us to the chairs.

Susan continues with her presentation, giving detailed information about each stage of labor. "A lot of time during contractions," she says, "you're going to have bowel movements. Don't be embarrassed. You're not the first, and you won't be the last. There will be a whole pad of gauze under you, which the nurse will fold up and dispose of after you."

Swell. That's just swell. I sit there, staring at the images on the screen. All I can think is, *How Did This Happen to Me?*

Matt is leaning against my locker after school the next day. "Are you still mad?" he asks.

I shoot him a look.

"I have to be at work by 4:30," he says. "Can I give you a ride home?"

I think about saying something sarcastic about Lauren. I saw them talking at his locker earlier today.

"Look, I'm sorry about the other day," he says. "But we should talk."

He doesn't look that sincere, but I want to believe him. I really do. Besides, we have a baby to think of. "Okay."

We're sitting in his car at a stoplight when he says, "I got that full-time construction job." He's staring straight ahead, his eyes fixed on the light. "So maybe we should start looking for apartments."

"Hey, that's great." I touch his arm and think that maybe we'll be okay, that everything will work out. The light turns green, and he keeps his eyes on the road the rest of the way home. His mouth is tight and grim.

I remember what Kelly had said about getting pregnant to trap Matt. When he pulls into the driveway, I turn to him. He doesn't bother to put the car in park. "Matt, do you think I did this on purpose?" I ask. There's no way he'd think that, but I want to hear him say so.

He looks impatient. "Do *what* on purpose?"

"Get pregnant."

He shrugs. "It hardly matters now."

"What does that mean?"

"Never mind. It doesn't matter," he says.

"I didn't do this to trap you." I promised myself I wouldn't cry, but the tears start flowing anyway. "How could you even *think* I'd do something like that? I wanted to have an *abortion* at first, remember? I didn't want to get pregnant!" I can tell by the look on his face that he's not entirely convinced.

He doesn't respond. Instead, he looks at his watch and says, "Ali, I'm going to be late."

I barely close the door of his car when he tears off.

⁓

"How can you go on like this?" Monica asks over the phone that night. "You guys aren't getting along at all, but you're still going through the motions. It's like you're both paralyzed."

"It's complicated." But this voice inside me asks, *Is it really so complicated?* I want to do the right thing, but I'm not even sure what that is any more. Before we hang up, I ask about Kyle. "What's going on with you guys?"

"You won't believe this. Mom has totally backed off. So has Steve."

"Seriously?"

"She says she can't keep us apart, so she's not going to try."

"Wow."

"I know. Best of all, Kyle will be living at home this summer, so we can see each other every day."

⁓

Ms. Connor is in her office Friday morning. She's drinking coffee and picking at a blueberry muffin.

"Are you busy?" I ask.

"No. Come on in."

I shut the door and sit in the green vinyl chair next to her desk.

"What's on your mind?" she asks.

"It's about Matt. You know, he gives me this ring and says he wants to get married, and now he's gotten this job where he can work construction full-time after graduation, but it's like he's mad at me, like this is all my fault. I'm due in six weeks, and I don't know . . ." I almost tell her about Lauren, but then I don't. "Do you think you could talk with him?" I keep thinking that if he just came in, maybe things would get better. Ms. Connor never gives me advice, but always insists that I set goals, and goals are what Matt and I need.

"Sure, I can talk with him," she says. "Why don't you bring him with you next time?"

On Monday, we finish reading *Hamlet*. Finally, a light at the end of the tunnel—or so we thought. But Carrot Top then brings out the sacred text again and asks what we think of Hamlet as a man. Someone coughs, everyone starts paging through the book, but no one says a word. Carrot Top looks personally offended. She reminds us that this is an *Advanced Placement* English class. Finally, Niles says, "He's a mass of contradictions." It's the first time he's said anything in class all semester.

Carrot Top smiles. "Yes," she says. "Go on."

"The dude doesn't know who he is," he says. "He doesn't believe in himself or in God, so he defines himself by his circumstances. In his mind, he's the dude whose mother married his uncle—the guy who murdered his father."

"*Yes, yes, yes,*" says Carrot Top. She's really excited now. "Hamlet has no center. He's the man who thinks too much, who can't make up his mind, who never wholly commits to anything."

Later that day, I look for Matt right before lunch. We didn't have a chance to talk during study hall, and I want him to see Ms. Connor with me. But as I turn down the small corridor near his locker, I see Lauren leaning against it, as if she belongs there. Then Lauren sees me, our eyes meet, and I turn away.

I eat with Monica at lunchtime. Monica is eating a bean burrito, the special of the day. I have a cheese sandwich, which I haven't touched yet.

"Oh, I got some pictures back yesterday," Monica says, reaching into a pocket in her backpack. "There's one of you and Matt." She sorts through them until she finds it and hands it to me.

I remember when she took it—before spring break at my house with a disposable camera. I was sitting on one end of the sofa, Matt on the other. My hair is pulled back, and I'm smiling directly into the camera, but it's a forced smile. Matt's arm is resting on the back of the sofa, but he looks stiff, and he's staring at me with a sort of bewildered expression on his face. That's when it hits me. *Neither of us looks happy.*

Maybe Monica's right. Maybe we *are* only "going through the motions." One night, when we weren't fighting for a change, we went to a movie and then drove to our usual place and parked. Matt touched and kissed me in all the familiar ways, but I knew he wasn't really there. Afterward, when I was already back home, it occurred to me that he never said, "I love you." That isn't like him at all.

❧

In photography class, we can come and go as we like now. I'm in the lab developing a couple rolls of film. Mr. G. comes by to check on my work. He laughs when he sees the photograph of Monica sticking out her tongue, and smiles when I show him the photo of my dad nose-to-nose with the retriever. But then when he sees the photograph of my mom, which I don't think is that great, he studies it closely and asks, "Who's this?"

"My mother."

He considers it for a while. "She looks pensive . . ." he says, "worried, but it's almost as if she's trying to mask it."

Matt doesn't come with me to see Ms. Connor. He says he doesn't have time.

I relay this to Ms. Connor on Wednesday while I help myself to a lemon drop from her jar. She looks at her notepad, as she always does, and considers this for a while.

"I don't know what to do any more," I say. "It's like he keeps saying 'Let's make this work. Let's get married.' But he's not doing anything to make it happen."

"Sometimes a person's actions speak volumes," she says.

"What do you mean?"

"Consider his actions in all of this, Ali. By not doing anything, he's telling you something. By not doing anything, he's also making a choice."

Before I leave, I ask Ms. Connor if she's married. "I'm a widow," she says, "going on two years now. He was really sick. He died when Zoe was a baby."

"Is it hard—being a single parent?"

"Extremely," she says. "But I can't imagine my life without her."

"May I ask you one other thing?"

"Sure."

"What would you do if you were me?"

"Ali . . ." she says, "you have to make your own decisions.

There are times in life when you won't like any of your choices, but you still have to make a decision."

❦

On Saturday afternoon, I go over to Kelly's apartment to babysit Erica. I wish I'd never promised. I've been really nervous because I've never taken care of a newborn before, but it's not so hard. Erica sleeps for more than an hour in her infant seat on the living room floor while I work on my English paper about *Hamlet*.

Kelly told me that Erica would probably sleep most of the afternoon, but at 2:00, she wakes up screaming. I try rocking her to calm her down. That doesn't work. Then I hold her close and pace the living room. That doesn't work either. I check Erica's diaper—bone dry. Finally, I remember the bottle of formula Kelly left for her in the refrigerator. A cartoon bubble forms over my head. *"Eureka!"* Erica settles down at once, sucking hard on the bottle, and snorting loudly.

"You were just hungry, weren't you?" Erica studies my face with big eyes. After she drinks the bottle, I burp her, giving myself a mental pat on the back for remembering to burp her. Babies aren't that hard. I can do this. I place Erica back in her infant seat and get back to my paper, but I haven't written a single sentence when Erica screws up her face and howls. She turns this bright purple-red shade, and I'm afraid her head will pop off. Then there's this *rumble . . . rumble . . . phooosh*. Major blowout. There's poop exploding out of her diaper, though she's wearing the new and improved brand with "leak-guard protection," and I get it all over my arm.

I can't study the rest of the afternoon. For reasons unknown, Erica cries for two solid hours. Then she finally falls asleep, probably from sheer exhaustion.

By the time Kelly arrives, I'm totally wiped out. I don't bother telling her how awful the afternoon was. Kelly walks in with this big smile on her face. "I got a job as a cashier!" she announces. "I can work evenings, when Jar gets off work, and I'll be taking home about $100 a week!" She makes it sound as if she just won the lottery.

"That's great," I say, trying to sound positive.

When I get home, I find Mom in her studio, painting another African basket.

"How'd it go with Erica this afternoon?"

"Okay." I'm not about to admit how hard it was. If I do, Mom will go into this whole lecture about whether I want to keep the baby and how I'm about to completely tank my life.

I'm on my way downstairs when she calls out, "Ali, Matt called. He's planning to stop by after work."

At 5:30, Matt rings the doorbell, and I open the door right away. I've been waiting for him. I'm even wearing the ring he gave me at Christmas.

"Hi," he says, but he doesn't come in or kiss me hello the way he used to when we first started going out. He looks at me for a second, in a way that makes me feel jumpy inside, then he says, "Let's go somewhere."

I pull on my denim jacket and call to Mom that I'll be back in awhile. We drive around, and then he parks the car on some back road we've never been to before. I rub the pad of my thumb over the ring. I'm not used to wearing it, and even though it looks right on my hand, it feels strange.

He turns toward me and glances at my hand. A muscle flicks at his jaw. "I called Al . . . I told him I won't be taking that construction job after all. I accepted at Pratt." He doesn't look at me when he says it.

He looks out the window and fiddles with his car keys.

"What are you saying?" A wave of panic sweeps through me.

All this time, I felt he would bail on me, and now it's happening.

"I know it was my idea to get married and raise the baby ourselves. But I've thought about it a lot, and I just don't see how we can make this work. The construction job pays pretty well, but it'll barely cover our rent and food. There wouldn't be much left over for tuition and all the other expenses, and my mom and dad aren't going to help us, Ali. I think we should stick with our original plan. Give the baby to the Gardners and go to college."

"You want to give our baby up?"

"Look, Ali, the Gardners can give this baby so much more than we can right now. Be realistic. It's the only way. If we keep the baby, everyone's life is ruined. Mine, yours, and the baby's."

"It's so simple for you, isn't it? It must be nice to walk away from this, without a second thought."

"Ali . . . it's the only way."

I want to ask him about Lauren, but my throat squeezes shut. I close my eyes. *Breathe*, I tell myself. *Breathe, breathe, breathe.* Maybe Lauren's the real reason behind all this. Maybe if I hadn't gotten pregnant, things would be different, but there's no going back. Everything has changed. I open my eyes and look at Matt. I can tell he's already checked out. We've been together for more than a year, and been through so much together, but suddenly nothing about him seems familiar any more. Neither of us says anything on the drive home. When he pulls into the driveway, I open the door and step out.

He leans over, and I'm somewhat shocked to see tears in his eyes. "I know you don't think so, but I really loved you. It's just that . . . I can't do this, Ali. I can't."

I take off the ring and hand it to him. "Don't do this to us," I want to say, but the words stay stuck in my throat. Matt doesn't look at the ring. He tosses it in the cup holder, then looks at me for a minute before turning away. *I really loved you*—past tense. How can he shut off his emotions just like that? I close the door, and something closes off in my heart. Matt is the last person on earth I ever thought would let me down.

Chapter 21

When I was twelve years old, I couldn't wait to fall in love. Never once did I consider the trouble love can bring. I can't eat. I can't sleep. So I cry and remember every kiss, every touch, every moment we ever shared together. I'm well aware of how pathetic I am, but I miss him. It's a letdown to just be the old me again. I liked the person I was when I was with Matt. I'm not ready to let that go.

The first week, I sulk in my room, lying on my bed, staring at the ceiling. And though I'm not hungry, I manage to choke down some cheese puffs. I want to call him, but every time I pick up the phone, something stops me. I think about saying something to Monica about it, but she'll spaz if she knows I'm even *thinking* about calling Matt.

I don't tell my parents right away, but when I finally do, my mom says "Oh, honey, I'm sorry." She looks as if she might actually mean it. My dad gives me a hug. But neither of them looks that surprised. My dad worries I'm not eating enough, so he makes me smoothies every day, and every night before I go to sleep, he comes in and asks me how I'm doing.

When I get bored with being pathetic, I get angry. Matt has let me down in the worst possible way. How can he just walk away? Doesn't he care about me? About the baby? Whatever we had was most definitely not love. It's over, really over, and I'm glad to have him out of my life and out of my heart. I rip up his photo—the one I kept tucked in the mirror on my dresser. I don't look for him at school, or call him at home, or even stop by the store where he works for so much as a pack of gum. He's no longer in second period study hall, and I have a new lunchtime strategy—avoid Matt. Sometimes, Monica and I pick up something in the cafeteria and eat in her car with the windows rolled down. Sometimes we skip out altogether and go for tacos. The strategy works. I don't see Matt for several weeks. As far as I'm concerned, he no longer exists. He's no more than a speck of dust.

Then one day, from a distance, I see him in the school parking lot, and we make eye contact. I decide to be completely, totally cool. Not that it works. My knees go weak, my palms get clammy, and my heart starts pounding. I must be an idiot to feel this way.

I stay home from school the next day. I need a mental health day. My mother understands. She calls in and tells the school secretary that I have diarrhea. At first, I want to kill her, but then we both crack up. We're getting along better these days.

The yearbooks arrive at the beginning of May. Everyone on the yearbook committee distributes them at a table in front of the principal's office. The first dozen pages are all impromptu shots of *(surprise, surprise)* the cheerleaders and jocks and everyone on the yearbook committee. Monica goes through it page by page, looking for her picture, the way she does every year. But once again, she's been snubbed. There's one small photo of me working on *The Voice*. Fortunately, I'm behind my desk, so you can't tell I'm pregnant. The only picture of Monica is her class photo, and she looks really great, except for the fact that someone blacked out her front teeth and inserted a birthmark on her cheek. Monica slams her yearbook shut. *Those bitches.*

The prom is next week. The theme is "Starlight," and the

decorating committee plans to transform the cafeteria into para-
dise with white Christmas lights and two hundred gold and silver
stars—one representing each high school senior. Because it's such
a major job, they've already started hanging stars from the ceiling.

Everyone's talking about who bought dresses in Chicago,
where to meet for pre-prom drinks, and the best restaurants to
go for dinner. The school board arranged for an after-prom party
at the mall, but I don't think anyone's planning to show up. Sarah
Vogel (head cheerleader, queen bee) scores a prom date with Austin Geery, captain of the football team (cute, muscular, but not
too bright). The date's all she talks about in Carrot Top's class.
The way she keeps going on, you'd think she was planning her
wedding. I can't believe it's taken them four years to find each
other.

Like me, Monica's never really been into the prom thing. But
now that she's with Kyle, she's become sickeningly romantic and
is seriously considering asking Kyle to prom. I'm her sounding
board for three days and listen to all the pros and cons ad nause-
am, but in the end, Monica decides against it for two reasons. A.)
She's fairly certain a college freshman wouldn't be caught dead
at a high school prom. And B.) This would send her mother—who
pretends to understand about Monica's "special friendship" with
Kyle—completely over the edge.

School's a waste of time. No one's paying attention in class or
turning in homework. The girls keep cutting classes for appoint-
ments at the tanning salon, and the boys are rowdier than usual.
The Wednesday before prom, some guys—mostly Jocks and Stoners—start a food fight in the cafeteria and knock down fifty-two
"Starlight" stars from the ceiling with mashed potatoes. I think
the authorities should cancel school the week before prom.

In response to a request by Student Council for a scheduled Senior Skip Day, the principal announces over the intercom on Monday that "while the request was taken under consideration, it was deemed inappropriate." The seniors take matters into their own hands, and by Wednesday that week the unofficial "Senior Skip Day" is set for Friday at Willow Lake. Personally, I could use another day off, but I don't feel up to a day at the beach. I would rather stay home and rearrange my comb drawer. But on Friday morning, Monica shows up at 10:30, wearing a pink T-shirt and cutoffs, her sunglasses parked on her head. She insists we go to the lake because she wants to work on her tan. My mother is happy to see her maladjusted daughter finally get out of the house. She packs us lunch in a picnic basket and practically pushes me out the door.

As soon as we get to the lake, Monica puts on her bikini and pops open a beer. She hands me a bottle of sparkling water, cherry flavored. "For you and the baby," she says. Then she slathers Banana Boat suntan lotion all over her body, pulls on her cat-eyed sunglasses with pink rhinestones, and lays back to catch the rays. She takes tanning very seriously. I sip my water, wearing my maternity shorts and t-shirt. Looking like Buddha with my stomach on my lap, I wonder if I'll ever be skinny again.

I try to relax and enjoy the sun. I lean back on Monica's pink-and-yellow striped blanket, trying to find a position that's comfortable, and together we watch the sunlight glitter across the water like diamonds. She turns to me and asks, "Are your breasts still getting bigger?"

"I think so," I say.

"Wow, I didn't think that was possible."

Her cell phone rings three times in an hour. I know it's Kyle. Every time he calls, she lowers her voice, grins stupidly, and sighs. They've been seeing each other exclusively since spring break, and Monica is on the pill. I miss the old Monica—the one who went out with someone new every few weeks.

"I'm starving," Monica says after the last call and starts rummaging through the picnic basket. "Wow, is that chicken salad?" She pulls off the wax paper and starts to chow down. Then she finds a container my mother packed. "Is this your mom's guacamole?"

"I think so."

She pops off the lid, and uses corn chips to scoop up the guacamole. She's about halfway through her sandwich, and most of the way through the guacamole, when she looks up at me and says, "Why aren't you eating?"

"I'm not really hungry," I say, but I grab a sandwich anyway and take a small bite.

She studies me for a moment. "What's *wrong* with you?" she asks, popping open another beer.

"Nothing." I take another bite of my sandwich. A few other people from school show up. Someone starts a volleyball game, and I start scanning the beach for Matt. "Have you seen Matt lately?" I ask Monica, as if he hasn't been on my mind all day.

Monica pulls off her sunglasses and looks at me. "*Aren't you over him yet?*"

I choose not to respond. Responding will only get me into trouble. I shrug and look away.

"I don't know *why* you waste your time thinking about him," she says. "He's not worth it."

By late afternoon, half the senior class is on the beach. Sarah Vogel is there with her entourage and all the jocks. Robin Evans, Amy Kassin, and the rest of the burnouts smoke dope at the picnic tables. Andy and Natalie sit on a blanket, looking like they've been married for ten years. Sarah keeps following Austin Geery around like a puppy, and he keeps trying to lose her. Poor Sarah— she doesn't get it.

Just before we leave, Monica uses the bathroom to change back into her clothes, and Niles shows up with Nick Pedraza, who immediately heads over to the picnic tables to get stoned. Niles waves when he sees me, then walks over and sits on the blanket next to me while I scoop up handfuls of sand and pour them into a pile.

"So how's it going?"

"Okay."

He looks at me for a minute, then away. "I heard about you and Matt . . . Sorry . . . That's tough." He downs the last of Monica's beer. "What you're doing, though," he says, "having this baby . . . is very cool. You're the bravest chick I know." Then he raises his arm to give me a high five, but instead of slapping my hand, he squeezes it. The star is still there on his wrist—with Tory's name right next to it.

He's already gone when Monica gets back from the restroom. She tosses me her keys. "I'm so buzzed," she says. "You drive."

I scan the beach one more time before we leave. Matt never shows up, but Lauren Thompson does. We walk right past her when we pack up to leave. She got her nose pierced. There's a pink stone on the left side of her nose, which I know Matt would hate. "I can see getting your belly button pierced," he said once, after doing a sketch of Robin Evans, who wears one, "but your nose? I don't get it." Just thinking about it makes me smile.

❧

Finally, it's the last week of school. The entire photography class is outside shooting pictures of the school and each other. I'm sitting on the grass, my stomach in my lap, taking a break, when Mr. G. picks up my camera and takes a shot of me, looking like a beached whale.

"What are you doing?" I say.

"Capturing this moment on film. Believe me, you'll appreciate it someday. You can look back and remember what you looked like."

"Thanks," I say, but it's hard to imagine wanting to remember this moment. Afterward, Ms. Connor walks by, calling out to me, waving, then talking with Mr. G. I can't make out what they're saying, but you can tell they're really into each other. There's something about the way he looks at her, and the way she smiles and touches his arm before leaving. I like the idea of the two of them together.

Next period, Mrs. Danker tells me she'd like my last column to be "something more personal," which is her way of saying that my last four columns have *really* sucked. They read like news articles. I try two or three different ideas, but they're all disasters. Then one day, I'm on my way to the parking lot with Monica, and I see Niles in the parking lot with Nick Pedraza and a few other guys. Niles is leaning against the hood of this guy's car, and someone says something to him that makes him throw back his head and laugh out loud. I haven't seen him like that since before the accident, which I still can't forget about.

That night, I start writing, and for the first time in months, the words start flowing. I write about senior year and staring our future in the face. I write about how everything changes: how each of us has us a story to tell; how we're always forming new relationships and altering existing ones; how we're in a constant state of revision, turning everything inside out. It's the first thing I've written all year that I'm really proud of. I try a few different headlines, but nothing works. Then, in the middle of the night, one comes to me: "Inside Out."

Chapter 22

Graduation Day is sunny and hot. And though it's 92 degrees, with humidity of 72 percent, it practically takes an act of Congress to get my father to turn on the air conditioner. The baby was due last week. I'm beginning to think it's never going to come out. But on Graduation Day, I wake up feeling charged. I clean my room, start a load of laundry, and make lemon bars from scratch. I'm on a roll.

My mother hasn't exactly been enthusiastic about setting up a nursery in our house. Instead, she borrows a portable crib from the hospital and tells me we can set it up in my room to start. She doesn't say so, but I know she's hoping I'll change my mind and give the baby up. "Keep your options open" is how she likes to put it.

Later that morning, I'm standing in the laundry room folding clothes when Mom comes in from her morning walk.

"Mmm. What smells so good?" she asks.

"Lemon bars." I feel this menstrual-like cramp, and put my hand on my stomach, but it's gone a minute later.

"Are you okay?" Mom asks. She's frowning.

I nod. "It was just a twinge—same as I've been having off and on for weeks."

"You may be in labor, Ali. Maybe you should take it easy and rest."

"I don't think so."

I keep busy the rest of the day. For a while, I work with Mom in the garden, planting a border of lavender and watching a yellow butterfly.

I'd swear that butterfly was following me. It flutters from plant to plant, but stays close to me the entire time. It lands once directly on my arm and stays there for a long while, as if it's watching me. Later that afternoon, I run errands. I'm at a store buying shampoo when I feel this pressure in my stomach, and have to stop to catch my breath. When I get home, I take out my notes from childbirth class that describe the first phase of labor, but I have only one symptom.

"Are you sure you want to go to graduation?" Mom asks.

"Sure. Why not?"

I could have had my diploma mailed to me, and I seriously considered it, but Monica talked me into going to graduation. "Who cares what other people think?" she said. It isn't like I have anything better to do. Besides, the gown I have to wear is as big as a tent. You can hardly tell I'm pregnant in it. But the *real* reason I want to go is that Matt will be there. The pathetic truth is I want to see him, even if it's only from a distance. I still think about him all the time.

Monica is stopping by at 5:00 to pick me up. Mom, Dad, and Aunt Laura are planning to leave a little later. So I take a shower and wash my hair, but twice I have to sit down. By 4:00, the contractions are coming regularly, but I still don't believe they're for real. I go to my room and put on the cream-colored maternity dress Mom bought me.

When I finally come downstairs, Aunt Laura is already there. She brought Peter, the new guy she's dating. He's tan and blonde and has an earring in one ear. He takes my hand and says, "So you're Allison. I've heard so much about you."

Mom sets out a plate of cheese and crackers, and Dad uncorks a bottle of sparkling cider. They make a toast and then let me open my presents. Mom and Dad, who give me a new watch, take pictures. Aunt Laura gives me a leather backpack. Then they convince me to put on my cap and gown for more pictures. I don't feel like it, but they insist. So there I am, standing next to the fireplace saying "cheese" for the umpteenth time when I have a contraction so strong I have to sit down. Fifteen minutes later, I have another one that takes my breath away.

There's no way I'm going to graduation.

Mom calls Dr. Bishop, who says we can stay home until the contractions are seven minutes apart. When Monica stops by to pick me up, I'm in the driveway with Aunt Laura and Peter. I've already changed into my maternity jeans and one of my dad's white, V-neck t-shirts. They're going to walk with me for a while to help move the labor along.

Monica can't believe that it's actually happening—that I'm going into labor and missing graduation because of it. Before she leaves, Monica asks, "Do you want me to tell Matt?" which kind of surprises me because whenever she refers to Matt lately, the word "jerk" usually follows.

"Sure." We haven't talked since the day we broke up. He doesn't even look my way when we pass each other in the hall at school. Once, I sort of waved, but he turned the other way, as if he didn't see me, but I know he did. I hate that. Still, he has a right to know. He's the baby's father.

One hour passes, then another, and I'm tired of walking. My contractions are coming eight minutes apart.

"We're going to the hospital," Dad says.

I'm about to tell him I can wait, but then I get another contraction, and this time it's more intense. I grab Dad's hand and squeeze it hard.

~❧~

Dad drops Mom and me off at the emergency entrance to St. Mary's Hospital, then goes to park the car. After we register, an attendant appears with a wheelchair and insists I sit in it, even though I can walk. He takes Mom and me to the maternity ward, where a nurse with dark brown hair meets us.

"I'm Erin," she says, flashing a smile. She's wearing bright purple scrubs and a sweater. Erin wheels me into a birthing room, and she mentions on the way that she has five children of her own. This puts me at ease right away because I figure if she's been through this five times, she's something of an expert. Erin hands me a gown. "You'll need to put this on. Then I'll be back to check on you."

When Erin comes back, she pulls on rubber gloves. "I just want to see how far your cervix is dilated," she says. "Lie back and try to relax." Afterward, she pulls off her gloves and says, "Three centimeters." She smiles as if this is good news.

"*Three centimeters?* Is that all?" I was sure I'd be farther along than that.

"You can try walking if you like. That may help speed things along," she suggests.

When Dad finally gets there, we walk the maternity floor halls together. We keep it up for more than an hour. Whenever we turn the corner by the elevators, and the doors open, I half expect to see Matt. If there's anyone in the entire universe I want to see now, it's him. If he knows I'm in labor, he'll come. I'm certain of it. But every time the doors slide open, no Matt. Maybe Monica hasn't had a chance to tell him yet.

When my water breaks, it comes out in one big gush, drenching my slippers and splashing Dad's new shoes. We both laugh, though Dad looks as nervous as I suddenly feel. He walks me back to my room and makes a coffee run.

"I think we should call the Ryans and let them know you're here," he says before leaving. "Is that okay with you?"

My eyes fill with tears, my throat gets all tight, and all I can do is nod.

I get in the bed and try to get comfortable. Mom takes my hand and squeezes it. "You're doing great, sweetheart," she says. We don't talk much, but just having her there makes me feel better. I try to sleep, but I can't. I'm a little scared, and I keep thinking of Matt. Monica must have told him by now—it's after midnight. For a crazy minute, I wonder if he's with Lauren. Could he be that big of a jerk? I imagine Lauren and Matt, laughing together at a graduation party, holding hands and kissing. This isn't helping at all. Just thinking of them together makes me nervous and jumpy inside. I close my eyes. *Think beach. Think sand. Think warm sunny day.*

Mom is still holding my hand when I feel a wave of pain invade my body. It's the worst pain I've ever felt. "Breathe," Mom says. "*In* three seconds, *out* three seconds." She demonstrates. I focus on her and follow her instructions. *Breathe in, one, two, three. Breathe out, one, two, three.* I've forgotten everything I learned in childbirth class.

Dad walks in carrying two cups of coffee. "No one answered, so I left the Ryans a message on the machine," he announces. He hands one cup to Mom, sits in a chair next to the bed, and does the breathing exercises with us. They both look ridiculous.

At three in the morning, Erin comes in again to check me. She pulls on rubber gloves and asks how I'm doing. Dad excuses himself and leaves the room. "Six centimeters, and you're 90 percent effaced. Do you want something for the pain?" she asks.

"Yes." We've already discussed what type of painkiller to use. Erin leaves and comes back right away. She's holding something in her hands—the painkiller, I hope. I watch as she injects the medication into the IV in my arm, then I close my eyes. The pain is bad, but it's not as unbearable as I thought it might be—not yet, anyway.

The next hour goes by slowly, but the painkiller takes the edge off right away. Finally, I feel myself relax between contractions. Dad, stroking my head, sits behind me and tells me the story about the night I was born. The contractions are much stronger now. I kind of groan, but I'm not screaming like pregnant women always do on TV.

"You're doing great," Dad says. He wipes my forehead with a moist washcloth.

Dr. Bishop comes in, wearing green scrubs and a mask over her face. After examining me, she says, "It won't be long now."

I feel another contraction beginning. With my mom, I inhale and exhale slowly. My legs are beginning to tremble, and I feel really scared, but I won't let myself go there. When Erin checks me again, I'm at ten centimeters.

All of a sudden, the door to my room swishes open, and two nurses roll in a cart draped with a sheet. They uncover it, and I see all sorts of instruments. I feel another pang of pain, and suddenly the urge to push is strong. The doctor takes over the coaching. "Bare down and pushhhh."

I push through each contraction, with Dr. Bishop, Erin, and my mom urging me to push an extra second or two each time.

"You're doing great," says the doctor. "Okay, push, again, a little more, a little more, a little more. Keep pushing."

"You're doing great. Just great," Erin says. "Okay, are you ready again? *C'mon, c'mon, c'mon.* You're almost there."

I push and rest, push and rest. Sweat is trickling down my neck, and just when I'm sure I can't handle the pain one more minute, the doctor says, "Okay, Ali, one more good push should do it." I grit my teeth and push as hard as I can, and finally, I feel the baby slide out.

"It's a boy," says the doctor. It's 5:06 in the morning. She holds the baby up, then snips the cord. His head is full of dark hair, and his body is reddish-blue and covered in some slimy mucus, which the nurse wipes away with a cloth. He makes tiny noises, his legs and arms flailing, and then he lets out a loud, lusty howl and doesn't stop. The nurse weighs him and puts a band around his ankle while I watch from the bed.

I thought I would feel something right away—a rush of love or a strong connection. But I don't. I feel removed from the experience, as if I'm watching it happen to someone else.

"Does he have a name yet?" Dr. Bishop asks.

"Jonah," I say, thinking back to Christmas when Matt and I had discussed it.

"That's a great name," says one of the nurses. "And what's his middle name?"

It was going to be Matthew, but that was when Matt and I were planning to get married, so now I don't know. I shake my head. Mom glances at me, then back at the nurse. "Can we wait on a middle name?" she asks.

"Sure," says the nurse. She writes "Jonah Parker" on a card with a black-felt marker and tapes it to the bassinet they wheeled in for the baby.

While Dr. Bishop stitches me up, I stare at the ceiling. Dad, saying something about calling Aunt Laura, slips out of the room. Mom is holding the baby now, and tears are streaming down her face.

When the doctor finishes, Mom sets the baby in the crook of my arm. He's wrapped tightly in a blanket and has a soft blue cap on his head. I still feel shaky, but I hold onto him carefully. He's so fragile, and he smells so new.

"Hello," I whisper, and he opens his eyes and looks at me as if he somehow recognizes me. He has dark hair, like Matt's, and perfect tiny red lips.

Erin squeezes my arm and flashes a big smile. "Good job, Mom. We'll leave you alone for a while."

Mom . . . Mom . . . I'm a mother now. I thought that when I saw my baby or held him in my arms, I would feel different, but I don't. I'm just Allison Marie Parker . . . exhausted, shaky, and a little scared. I don't feel like anyone's mother.

Dr. Bishop and the nurses leave the room, but Mom stays with me.

"He looks like Matt," I say. He really does . . . his lips . . . his hair . . . the shape of his nose. But then I lift one tiny hand and examine his fingers, and they are shaped more like mine. I still can't believe he's really here. This is my son. I am his mother. *Me . . . a mother?*

❧

Later that morning, I wash my hair and put on a blue night-shirt I brought from home. All day, I'm sure Matt will visit us. He may hate me, but he'd want to see his baby. I'm certain he'll come by, but he never shows up, and it's hard—really hard. The maternity ward at St. Mary's is filled with noises. There's a chorus of babies crying, the chuckles of new fathers and grandparents, and the intermittent ping of a nurse's call bell.

Monica stops by and brings me a veggie sandwich from Java House and a silver toe ring with a butterfly on it. "I thought you might like it, now that you can see your feet again," she jokes.

"Thanks," I say, setting it aside for later. I don't feel like trying it on now.

A nurse rolls in the bassinet. The baby is awake, and Monica asks if she can hold him. She's surprisingly good with babies. He snuggles into her chest and falls right to sleep.

"He looks like Matt, doesn't he?" I say.

"Maybe a little," she says. Matt is not exactly her favorite person these days. When I ask whether she thinks Matt will stop by, Monica shrugs.

Later, a nurse takes the baby back to the nursery so a pediatrician can examine him. Mom and Dad go home to shower, promising to come back later. Then Monica leaves, and for the first time all day, I'm alone. I start wondering whether I'm really ready to be a mother, when Andy knocks on the door.

"Hey," he says.

"Hey." Andy's the last person I was expecting, but I'm glad he's here.

"I hope it's okay I'm here . . . I just wanted to see how you're doing. Monica told me the news," he says. He gives me a toy bear with a balloon that says "Congratulations!" tied to a paw.

Andy stays for an hour. He brings me a copy of the last issue of *The Voice*, with my last column, "Inside Out." I almost ask him about Matt, but I stop myself. Then he asks if he can see the baby, so we walk down to the nursery together and watch Jonah from the window.

After a while, he turns to me. "Are you keeping him?" he asks.

I try to choke out a "yes," but I can't, so I nod. Andy walks me back to my room. Before leaving, he starts to say something, but stops himself mid-sentence. Instead, he leans down and hugs me tightly.

An hour later, someone announces over the intercom that visiting hours have ended, and I know that Matt was serious when he said he wanted no part of this.

My mother stays the night with me, sleeping in the green recliner in the room, but it takes me a long time to fall asleep. I feel really sore, and all I can think about is whether I'm doing the right thing keeping Jonah.

When I finally fall asleep, I have this dream about Jonah. There he is, standing in a sunny field, and he's older, maybe three or four, when he starts to run away from me. He's happy and laughing. He turns to me and says, "It's okay, Mommy. I'll always love you." All of a sudden, he becomes a dove and soars higher and higher into the sky until he disappears. Then, I'm alone in the field, surrounded by butterflies fluttering all around me . . . beautiful butterflies in colors I've never seen before.

I can't get back to sleep after that. In the morning, when the light turns yellow and pale, Mom gets up and goes for coffee. As soon as she leaves, a nurse brings the baby to me and asks if I'm nursing. "Yes," I say. I've read how good breast-feeding is for the baby, and I want to give him the best start possible. The nurse takes a few moments to show me how again and then leaves.

It's the first time I'm alone with him. I feel awkward at first, trying to nurse him, but it's like he knows exactly what to do. He latches on to my nipple and sucks for ten minutes. It hurts a little, but I don't mind.

He falls asleep before he finishes, and I hold him in my arms and watch him. He starts to feel heavy, and my arms hurt a little, but I don't care. He's so sweet . . . so beautiful . . . but am I ready to be his mother? I was sure I could do this, with or without Matt, but I'm not so sure any more. I touch his silky hair, and his sweet baby smells shoot straight to my heart. He's still sleeping, but his lips curl into a smile, and I wonder what he's dreaming about. Something in my heart opens—a place I never knew was there before. I lean down and kiss him.

"I love you," I whisper, tears sliding down my cheeks.

Suddenly, all I can think about is the Gardners and their pretty white house, surrounded with flowers. It's so easy to picture him there on the front lawn, lying on a blanket, surrounded by a mother and father who love him. All this time, I've been thinking about how *I* could never give up my baby—about how awful it would make *me* feel. But maybe it doesn't matter how *I* feel. When I look at Jonah, the one thing I know for sure is that I want only what's best for him. And I can't give him that right now.

Later that morning, when I tell my parents what I've decided, it's my mother who asks if I'm "really certain" that's what I want. And she doesn't ask me once, but three times. My dad says, "Ali, I know this isn't a decision you made lightly. I think you're doing the right thing for Jonah, and I'm proud of you."

My mom waits until "a reasonable hour" to call the Gardners. She's worried about disturbing them too early in the morning, but we both know they wouldn't mind. At 9:00, she makes the call. I can hear her discussing the details with them on her cell phone outside my room, while a nurse checks my pulse and blood pressure. Dad is holding Jonah as if he were a china doll, studying his face and his hands. Before the nurse leaves, she tells me I should try breastfeeding him again, and when Dad brings him to me, he wipes tears from his eyes with the back of his hand. I've never seen my dad cry before.

My mother is still in the hallway, talking to the Gardners. "Yes," she says, "Ali is doing quite well, all things considered. We're all so happy for you . . . Okay, we'll see you tomorrow . . . Bye."

For the rest of the day, we take turns holding Jonah, commenting on how tiny and perfect he is. My mother keeps kissing the top of his head and wiping away her tears. My father sits in the chair, holding Jonah, and remarks about the size of his hands. For the first time, I consider how hard this is for them, too. My parents come up with all sorts of excuses to leave me and Jonah alone in the room. They go out for lunch, to get coffee, and to buy film at the gift shop. I'm glad they do. A nurse comes in every once in a while to take my blood pressure, but the rest of the time I hold him, committing every part of him to memory—the curve of his cheek, his soft downy hair, and the sounds he makes while he sleeps.

I wish I could tell Jonah why I have to let him go. I wish he were old enough to understand.

Later that afternoon, Mom tells me she's going home to shower and change, and she promises to come back tonight. Dad says he needs to get some paperwork done at home, but he'll be back first thing tomorrow.

Before they go, I ask Mom to bring me the pink photo box that's on my desk and to pick up some stationery at the store.

"Do you have anything special in mind?" she asks.

"Something with butterflies," I say, looking at Jonah and remembering my dream.

That evening, I'm coming out of the hospital bathroom, and Mom is sitting in the recliner holding Jonah, when a nurse comes to take him back to the nursery for the night.

I look at my mom, and she looks at me. "No," we both say at exactly the same time. Then my mother says, "Thanks, anyway, but we'd rather keep Jonah with us tonight."

I nurse Jonah again, and he falls asleep right away. My mother takes him for me, holds him in her arms, and watches him sleep. Then I pull out the stationery she'd brought me. The lavender paper has a pale green border and colorful butterflies in the background. I write "Dear Jonah," and then I'm at a complete loss for words. This is the most important letter I'll ever write, but I don't know where to begin. I wasn't aware I'd said that aloud, but then my mother says, "Start at the beginning."

So I write about the day I met Matt in the cafeteria. I write about how we fell in love, how Matt told me he loved me that day at Willow Lake, and how I had said it back. I tell Jonah that even though our love wasn't meant to last, the feelings Matt and I had for each other were real. I tell him about meeting Ellen and Tom that day in the diner and how much they wanted him from the start. I tell him that Matt knew, even before I did, that he would be better off with Ellen and Tom. I tell him that giving him up is the hardest thing I've ever done. I know there's so much I'll be missing—his first tooth, first words, first steps. I tell him that if I were older, things would be different, but I'm still growing up and have a lot to figure out. I don't have a lot to offer him right now. I tell Jonah I'll never forget him, and I'll always love him, and that I hope someday we'll meet again.

When I started this letter, I thought all along that I'd close it with "Love, Mom." But by the time I finish, it occurs to me that, while I'm the mother who brought him into the world, Ellen and Tom will be his real parents. So I write "xoxoxo" and sign it "Love, Ali" in my big loopy handwriting. Then, I look for the photo of Matt and me in the photo box.

Monica took it last summer, that day at the lake when Matt told me he loved me and I said it back. In the picture, Matt and

I are sitting in the sand, holding hands, smiling wide, and I remember thinking that we'd be together forever. It's my favorite
picture of the two of us, but I want Jonah to have it. I fold the
letter with the photo tucked inside, and place it carefully in the
envelope. I write "Jonah" on the front and draw a heart next to
his name.

⚜

The next morning, I'm in the chair next to the window, holding Jonah in my arms, wondering if I'm doing the right thing. I'm
about to tell my parents that I want to call the whole thing off
when Ellen and Tom walk quietly into the room holding hands.
As soon as they see Jonah, Ellen covers her heart with her hand
and says, "Oh, Ali . . . he's beautiful." Then she starts crying,
Tom pulls her close, and they both look at Jonah, blinking back
tears. I kiss the top of Jonah's head and give him a light squeeze
before handing him over to Ellen. Jonah stretches and yawns and
snuggles into the curve of Ellen's arm, looking like he's belonged
there all along.

Everything happens quickly after that. My father looks over
the papers that the Gardners' attorney had drawn up, giving them
guardianship of Jonah for the time being, and I sign them with a
blue ballpoint pen. My father explains that I'll sign the official
adoption papers later. Then the Gardners and my parents leave
the room for a few minutes so I can say my final goodbye to Jonah.
I hold him close, breathing in his sweet baby smells, and capture
a memory to keep forever. When I kiss him goodbye, he opens his
eyes and looks right at me, and I know everything is going to be all
right. The Gardners will give him more than I ever could.

Before we leave, I give the letter to Ellen and ask if she'll
give it to Jonah some day. "Of course," she says, her eyes filling
again. She starts to say something else, but her voice breaks and
she shakes her head. Then Tom gives me a hug and says, "Thank

you, Ali . . . for everything." His voice is thick with emotion, and he looks like he wants to say something more, but then he shakes his head and gives me a light squeeze.

We leave, and it's over, just like that. I didn't think giving up my baby would be so simple . . . so simple, and yet so hard. My father leaves first to bring the car around to the front entrance. I'm sitting in a wheelchair because the attendant insists I do, and Mom is beside me, holding my overnight bag. I'm thinking about how empty I feel leaving the hospital without my baby, when I hear a voice call "Ali." I look up, and Ellen is running down the hall towards me. She stoops down next to me and takes my hand in both of hers. Her eyes are red and watery, but I've never seen Ellen look happier. "Thank you," she whispers. "Thank you, from the bottom of my heart."

Three days later, on a cloudy Friday morning, I sign the official adoption papers at the court house in Lakeview. My parents offered to go with me, but I wanted to do this alone. My father has hired an attorney, and she meets me outside the court house. Her name is Jane Carmen, and she reminds me a little of Aunt Laura. Before we go inside the judge's chamber, she tells me what's going to happen and goes over some of the forms with me.

The judge is an older man with gray hair and large, round glasses that make him look owlish. He asks if I'm on any drugs—legal or otherwise—that might cloud my thinking. He asks if anyone is paying me or forcing me to make this decision. I say "no" each time. Then he asks for identification, so I show him my driver's license. Just before I sign the papers, he leans forward in his chair and asks, "Are you very sure? Because once you sign this document, you can't change your mind. Your rights will be terminated."

"Yes," I say.

Afterward, the judge smiles at me with sympathetic eyes. Then he clears his throat and says, "Allison, you may feel badly now about placing your child with an adoptive family. But what you have done here today shows you're putting your baby's future first, and for that I commend you."

"Thank you," I say, but his words don't make me feel any better.

Jane gives me a copy of the papers I've just signed and a different set of papers for Matt to sign. Then we say goodbye on the court house steps. On the way to the parking lot, it starts to rain. I barely make it to my mom's car before it starts pouring. I quickly get in and then put the key in the ignition, but I don't start the car. I sit there, with the rain pelting against the windshield, and cry and cry . . .

⟶⟵

I think *Webster's Dictionary* should add, under the definition for "ambivalence," something about giving up your baby for adoption. Giving up your baby creates powerfully ambivalent feelings—it's probably the most selfless *and* the most selfish thing I've ever done, and it ignites a tug of war within me. My brain assures me that Jonah is where he belongs, but my heart makes me question myself for days. One morning, I'm having a really hard time. My brain and my heart can't stop bickering, and sometimes they switch sides. My brain, for instance, argues that Jonah would be better off with me because *I am his biological mother.* Then, my heart insists that this is about love, and Jonah deserves *two* parents who love him, not one.

The only peace I get is when I remember the dream I had that first night in the hospital, when Jonah turned into a dove and flew away, leaving me surrounded by butterflies. My heart assures me this was a sign, plain and simple, but my brain insists it was only a silly dream that didn't mean anything. So I pray for another sign that I did the right thing. My brain points out that I'm being a hypocrite because I hardly ever pray and never believed in signs before, but my heart cheers me on. I ask my brain to please shut up.

Later that same day, I'm at the bookstore in town with my dad. He's looking for a travel guide to take along on vacation. I wander around the store, and before I know it, I'm standing in the aisle lined with baby books. There in front of me is a book of baby names. I page through until I find Jonah's name, and there it is—a sign—on page 145.

Jonah: From the Hebrew "Yonah," meaning dove.

I see Matt once after I give up Jonah, and that's so he can sign the papers the attorney had given me at the court house. I meet him at Vincent's while he's on break. He looks really good.

I say, "Hi."

And he says, "Hi."

Then we walk to the bank across the street from Vincent's so he can have the papers signed and notarized. The notary is a woman with short brown hair and a big sunny smile, but when she looks over the papers, she becomes more serious. Matt doesn't bother to read the papers. He just signs his name, and then the notary adds her signature and seal.

Afterward, we go outside to a bench in front of Vincent's, and we sit there and look at each other.

"How are you doing?" he asks.

"Okay . . . I'm going to Northwestern this fall."

"Great." We look at each other for a minute, and then he says, "I got the full scholarship to Pratt, so I'm going there."

"Oh, that's great." I'm happy for him. "Well. . ." I say, standing up.

"Ali . . ."

"Yeah?"

"What does he look like?"

"He looks like you," I say, and thinking of Jonah makes me smile. "He's really beautiful. I have a picture for you." I wasn't sure I'd give it to him, but since he asked, I pull it from my purse.

Matt studies it carefully and smiles, then slips it into his shirt pocket, right next to his heart. We stand there, looking at each other. I want to tell Matt that I still love him—maybe I always will—and that I don't regret anything. After all, we made this beautiful baby together. But then a woman and her daughter walk by and sit on a bench next to us, and Matt says he has to get back to work.

"See you around," I say, starting to leave, but Matt reaches for my arm.

The next thing I know, he's hugging me tightly, and I know I'll remember that moment forever. With the sun shining down on us in the middle of the afternoon, anyone watching would think we were two young people who didn't have a care in the world. I'm the first to let go, but I know I'll never love anyone else exactly the way I loved Matt.

Epilogue

Five Months Later

The campus is practically deserted. It's homecoming week-end, and almost everyone is at the football game. Melissa, my roommate, invited me to come along with a group of friends, but I told her I had too much work to do. I've been at the library most of the afternoon, working on a paper that's not due for another month. The truth is, I just want to be alone.

Today, Theodore Jonah Gardner is five months old, and giving him up is the hardest thing I've ever done. The other hard part—the part I hadn't thought about before—was coming to terms with my decision. I never thought I was the kind of person who would give away my baby.

The first six weeks were awful. When my milk came in, my breasts were so hard and engorged that I wondered if God was punishing me. But a nurse told me that happens to all new moth-ers. When my milk dried up, the pain in my breasts went away. Still, I don't think the pain of giving away a child will ever go away completely.

Is it right to give your baby away? I don't know. Ms. Connor once told me that all you can do is make the best decision you can at the place where you are. I think about that a lot.

After I gave the baby to the Gardners, my parents and I went on a vacation. Dad rented a condo in Gulf Shores for two weeks. I went for long walks on the beach and thought about the baby, Matt, and my life. Then one morning, I woke up, and giving up my baby wasn't the first thing I thought about any more. When we came home from vacation, a letter from Ellen Gardner was waiting for me.

Dear Ali,

Thank you for a miracle of love and the chance at being a mother. Teddy's arrival has enriched our lives and made us a family.

We named him after his grandfather, Theodore, but Tom and I call him Teddy. In Hebrew, Theodore means "gift of God," and he is that to Tom and me. We kept Jonah as his middle name because we know you and Matt picked that name with love and care, and we want Teddy to always remember that.

The day Tom and I met Teddy in your hospital room was the most beautiful, magical moment of our life. We loved him so much at that moment that we couldn't possibly imagine loving him more than that. But each day we find ourselves loving Teddy even more, and each day, Tom and I are filled with gratitude and wonder for the gift of this child. God bless you always and know that you made our dream of having a family come true.

Love, Ellen

Inside the letter was a picture of Teddy. He has dark hair, blue eyes, and a big gummy smile that proves I did the right thing. He's the most beautiful baby I've ever seen. I keep his photo inside a box in my desk at school, and every once in a while, when Melissa's not there, I take it out and study it.

I used to think that everything in my life was just some coincidence, but Teddy changed all that. Last year, getting pregnant seemed like a terrible mistake. But when I look at his picture, it's hard to think of him as a mistake. How can a baby as beautiful as Teddy be a mistake?

⌒⌒

When I get back to the dorm, I check my mailbox. There's a thick pink envelope from Monica. As I walk up the three flights to my room, I open it. I can hear the phone ringing as I let myself in.

"Hello?"

"*Finally!*" Monica says on the other end of the line. "I've been trying to call you all afternoon. Are you okay? I know Teddy's five months old today . . . and I know it's still hard for you."

"Yeah, it is," I say. Monica always remembers. I haven't told anyone here about Teddy. I wanted to make a fresh start, but with my best friend, it's different. Monica is at the University of Illinois in Champaign-Urbana, which is three hours away. She hasn't declared a major yet, but she's taking a class in fashion retailing. We still talk several times a week. "What's new with you?" I ask, looking through the pictures she sent. They're photos of me and her at the lake, the week before we both left for school.

"Kyle and I broke up."

"What happened?" They'd been so serious all summer.

"We just decided to take a break. He hasn't been calling as much . . . and, well, there are a lot of cute guys here at school."

I don't know what to say.

"Say something," Monica says.

"I'm just surprised."

"I'm only eighteen, and it's kind of weird dating my brother."

"*Step*brother," I say, and we both laugh.

"Any cute guys at Northwestern?" Monica asks. "Besides Kyle, that is?"

I grin. Some things about Monica never change. "I haven't had time to notice."

"What?"

"I'm too busy."

"C'mon, Ali. There must be at least one cute guy there."

"Okay. There is one . . . Ethan . . . He's a sophomore." I met him the first week of school in my Intro-to-Journalism class. "He invited me to a party tonight."

"So go."

"I don't know." I'm not ready, at least I don't think so. But last week, I called a clinic near campus and made an appointment to discuss birth control. Next time (not that I can even imagine it right now) I want to be prepared. I told Ethan I was busy, but we exchanged phone numbers and e-mail addresses, and he told me to let him know if I changed my mind. I decide not to tell Monica any of this right now. She'll read too much into it.

"Look, he didn't ask you to marry him. He just invited you to a party."

"I know."

"Ali, it's been five months. You can't shut out the world for the rest of your life. Unless . . . ."

"What?"

"Never mind."

"Just say it."

"Are you still in love with Matt?"

Before I have a chance to answer, Melissa bursts in the room with three of her friends. They're so loud it's impossible to talk on the phone.

"What's going on?" Monica asks.

"Nothing. Can I call you back later?"

"Sure."

In all of Monica's pictures, we're just goofing around. But the last one is a picture of me, a close-up, that I didn't want her to take. And there, on the right side of the picture next to my head, is a flutter of wings, slightly blurred and so small I almost missed it. But when I really look at it, I realize what it is—a butterfly.

Melissa's friends are still in our room when I go for a run before dinner. After I had the baby, I started running to lose the extra weight I'd gained, and now I'm hooked. When I go outside, my feet hit the pavement, and I take off. I'm still thinking about what Monica said. Before leaving for school, I asked Aunt Laura if you ever get over your first love. She got this dreamy look in her eyes and said, "You never forget your first love, Ali. But you can get over him, and you will."

The sun is starting to fade, but I'm still running, moving so fast my feet don't seem to be touching the ground. At this very moment, I'm sure I must be flying. The wind is in my hair, and I don't ever want to stop. I've been waiting forever to feel like this. I'm ready to face the future. After all, there's not much you can do about the people you leave behind. When I turn a corner, I run into Ethan.

"Hey," he says and stops.

"Hey yourself," I call, but I'm not about to slow down yet. I reach out to touch his arm as I pass by. "Race you," I say, flashing a smile. I'm down the block and across a street before Ethan comes to his senses and sprints after me. I can hear him behind me, and I wonder if he'll ever catch up.

Chances are he will, if only because I'll throw myself onto the patch of green grass up ahead. Above us will be that beautiful maple tree with the rich, buttery leaves.

Acknowledgements

Many thanks to my publisher and editor, Bruce Bortz, for his encouragement and support and for taking a chance on a first-time novelist. Most of all, I thank him for believing in this book and stepping up to the plate to prove it. I also want to thank Carolyn Der at Bancroft Press for her discerning eye and for comments and suggestions that improved this book in its final form.

Grateful thanks to Madelon Matile for discussing the details of teenage pregnancy with me, for inviting me into her classroom, and for introducing me to several young women who generously shared their stories. Many thanks to adoption attorney, Sara Howard, and also to Vicki Osborn at Bethany Christian Services for taking the time to explain the adoption process in Illinois. A special thanks to everyone at Planned Parenthood, especially Beth Levine, Victoria Heckler, Elizabeth Talmont, and Lorie Spear for their insight and guidance.

And last, but certainly not least, a heartfelt thanks to the following people: my husband, Gary, and my sons, Daniel and Davis, for their love and endless support; my incredibly gifted friend, Imara, for her special guidance and counsel; my forever friend and perennial first reader, Jennifer McCarthy Jurgensmeyer, who has helped me with countless drafts; the other early readers of this book, Karen Hickam and Audrey Freidman, who helped in the very beginning when the idea for this book was just taking hold; and my parents, Warner and Ruth Negley, who taught me never to lose sight of my dreams.

About the Author

Karen Hart began writing as a teenager. She wrote for her high school newspaper and later majored in journalism at Illinois State University, where she also wrote for the campus newspaper, *The Daily Vidette*.

Since then, Hart has had more than 20 years of experience as a creative and technical writer and editor. She has worked in both corporate communications and public relations, developing a variety of award-winning media and publications, including magazines, newsletters, brochures, and videos. Most recently, she has worked on freelance writing projects, and magazines, such as *Sonoma Family-Life* and *Enlightened Woman*, have published her articles.

The seed of inspiration for *Butterflies in May* began forming in high school, but later took hold after the birth of her first son. Though she was a teenager a long time ago, she believes that some things—like first love, relationships, heartbreak, and letting go—never change.

She's currently working on a new novel, *The Colour of Love*, as well as a book about dreams with noted American psychic, Imara. Hart resides in Santa Rosa, CA with her husband, Gary, and two sons.

"As an educator and therapist, I've had the privilege of entering the world of those who feel lost—overpowered and overwhelmed by choices and consequences. *Butterflies in May* tells such a story as Ali Parker makes a difficult journey to discover answers that'll satisfy the integrity of her heart. It's a book about finding courage and strength in the face of sorrow and loss. It's also about the sacrificial gift of love that heals not just one heart, but many hearts."—LLOYD FRITZ, EDUCATOR AND MARRIAGE FAMILY THERAPIST, SANTA ROSA, CA

"Karen Hart's *Butterflies in May* is a compelling coming of age novel, and a captivating and frank new book. In this moving story of a young woman facing the dilemma of an unintended pregnancy, the author beautifully captures the emotions of first love, the roller-coaster ride of emotions when facing the dilemma of an unintended pregnancy, and the feelings evoked when romantic ideals clash with the realities of the ultimate decision. Hart's depictions of parents, friends, as well as health care providers are vividly drawn and are presented in a balanced and insightful manner. By presenting the kaleidoscope of complex emotions that surface as life-shaping choices are made, the book offers parents and teens a wonderful opportunity to talk and share, through book clubs, classrooms, and drama productions, and as a teaching tool in a number of community settings."—DR. CLAIRE D. BRINDIS, PROFESSOR OF PEDIATRICS AND HEALTH POLICY, UNIVERSITY OF CALIFORNIA AT SAN FRANCISCO

"*Butterflies in May* is a poignant novel that captures so many of the issues associated with teen pregnancy—adolescent sexual development, romantic relationships, reproductive rights, reproductive services for teens, family relationships, educational demands, and planning for the future. The reader accompanies the novel's main character, Ali Parker, through many of the decisions and emotions she faces after learning she is pregnant, as well as the emotions and reactions of her boyfriend, best friend, and family. Author Karen Hart thus creates a perfect resource for educators to use with youth, parents, and professionals who work with young people. The opportunities for critical discussion about the key issues and values appear on almost every page. Short of shadowing a pregnant teen through her pregnancy, there is no better way to find out what it's like to be a teenager faced with an unplanned pregnancy."—LORI A. ROLLERI, MSW, MPH, SENIOR PROGRAM MANAGER, ETR ASSOCIATES, A NATIONAL NON-PROFIT ORGANIZATION THAT CONDUCTS ADOLESCENT REPRODUCTIVE HEALTH RESEARCH, TRAINING, AND PROGRAM DEVELOPMENT, SANTA CRUZ, CA

"*Butterflies in May* soars right into the hearts of young and old readers alike. It takes you into an unparalleled journey through the life of an expectant teenager. Author Karen Hart does an exceptional job of pulling you right into the mind of an adolescent faced with a life altering decision: whether to have an abortion, keep her newborn, or give her baby up for adoption. *Butterflies in May* made me feel as if I was Ali (the expectant teenager). I got a better understanding of what it would be like if I were to become pregnant. With that information, I believe I'm even better equipped to teach my PSI (Postponing Sexual Involvement) class to pre-teens, who are curious about sex. I will definitely be using *Butterflies in May* as a teaching tool. This book is a must have for all families because it opens up channels of discussion. *Butterflies in May* has broken the chains of silence that have held this topic (teenage pregnancy) captive for years."—Crystalyn Thomas-Davis, PSI Teen Leader, Walnut Hills High School '07, Cincinnati, OH

"*Butterflies in May* depicts a very honest and heart wrenching story of the life, decisions, and relationships of a pregnant teenager. The uncertainty that Ali experiences regarding her choices in pregnancy and her accompanying feelings are so true to life. As a case manager at a home for pregnant teens, I see this situation with every girl who walks through our door. Karen Hart creates a wonderful story that can help any pregnant teen realize that what she is feeling and experiencing regarding her pregnancy is normal and felt by many who are in the same situation."—Courtney Smith, Case Manager at Bridgeway, A Home for Pregnant Teens, Lakewood, CO

"*Butterflies in May* is a wonderful story about a teenage girl who finds out she's pregnant. The story immediately captures the reader's attention because the characters are so real and their feelings so easy to relate to. The story offers a message that's extremely important in today's world. Though parents don't want their children exposed to discussions about sex, teens are constantly bombarded with the topic. While TV shows glamorize sexual activities, this book offers a very real picture of the consequences of being sexually active at a young age. Karen Hart has written the story in a way that allows the reader to become a part of Ali Parker's life. As the story progresses, readers may find themselves questioning their own feelings about sex, abortion, and adoption. Readers undoubtedly will find themselves devastated, excited, and confused as Ali experiences these emotions herself. (Because the story deals with teenage sexuality, students in junior high may need some guidance from their parents while reading the book.)"—Morgan Zerwas, Middle School Teacher, Santa Rosa, CA

"I think Ali Parker is a strong, brave woman who made the right decision for her and the baby. She kept her head up when things got tough and stuck through it. I really enjoyed this book. When Ali had to make hard decisions, I felt as if I was right there in the middle of the conversations, making some decisions with her. It was touching and had very strong points. I think this book is really helpful for teens and young teens because it shows the consequences of having sex and the complications you might have to go through.

It will also help teens understand that it is hard to have a baby when you already have plans and goals for your life. Thank you for giving me the chance to read this wonderful book."—VALADIA LEE, TEEN LEADER, POSTPONING SEXUAL INVOLVEMENT PROGRAM, 11TH GRADE, HUGHES CENTER PAIDEIA PROGRAM, CINCINNATI, OH

"As a former teacher of adolescents, I recommend *Butterflies in May* to any student faced with life-altering decisions. The book provides a catalyst for discussing a sensitive issue in the classroom because the characters represent many voices in the pro-choice/pro-life debate. Even students not personally touched by teenage pregnancy will learn from Ali's emotional roller coaster as she struggles to make the best choice for all involved. Karen Hart's writing will appeal to the adolescent reader."—LINDA WEDWICK, FORMER MIDDLE SCHOOL TEACHER, NOW ASSISTANT PROFESSOR, CURRICULUM & INSTRUCTION DEPARTMENT, ILLINOIS STATE UNIVERSITY

"This story of teen pregnancy takes the reader through both the mother and father's relationship, ambivalence, and the many difficult decisions that take place in a 10-month period surrounding Ali's pregnancy. Each decision involves a detailed intellectual, emotional, and relationship consideration. The book is instructive and moving because it tries to present the issue from the father and mother's relationship to each other. I like the counselor's advice that people make their decisions by their actions, more than by their words. Ali's most important decision is based on an often neglected realization that 'every child deserves the love of two parents.' *Butterflies in May* is an educational story that will teach teens how a teen pregnancy turns your life inside out."—CHRISTOPHER KRAUS, JD, MTS, ADOLESCENT ADVOCACY MANAGER, CINCINNATI POSTPONING SEXUAL INVOLVEMENT (PSI) PROGRAM

"This book is one of those rare novels that immediately engages the reader, taking you on a journey of the mind, body, and spirit, all the while providing valuable insight to an all too prevalent issue—teen pregnancy. The statistics are staggering, and they cross all educational, social, and economic levels. Yet teenagers, ruled by their emotions, still fall victim to the *it-won't-happen-to-me* syndrome. Karen Hart's realistic, sensitive, and compassionate approach to the subject enlightens without lecturing. A beautifully offered story, *Butterflies in May* should top the list of required reading for all high school students."—LORI FLADSETH, MIDDLE SCHOOL TEACHER, SANTA ROSA, CA

"I loved *Butterflies in May*. It addresses a major problem I see almost daily—an increasing number of pregnant teenagers. It accurately lays out the emotion-charged decision-making process the girls undergo. It portrays the teenage boys in just the ways I've come to observe. And I cried the last two chapters. May every teenager, boy or girl, get a chance to read this terrific book—before they, too, run headlong into the problem."—DR. ELLIE TAYLOR, GYNECOLOGIST, BALTIMORE, MD

"Ali's difficult decision—her decision-making process and what happens to her thereafter—is what this story is all about. The storyline is well told and very readable, at least from my observations of thirty-five years in the private practice of Obstetrics and Gynecology. The way the family moves from what was general support for the initial course of action to suggesting another direction, for better or worse, was quite realistic. The boyfriend's leaving after an initial commitment, is, in reality, what we see commonly. Also quite realistically described was the scene outside the clinic—I see this same scene outside our clinic every Saturday. (In our state, we have enacted 'Bubble Laws' for the patient's protection.) I regard *Butterflies* as an excellent springboard for discussions in high school, and even junior high, social studies, science, biology, and sexuality classes. Well done!"—DELL BERNSTEIN, M.D., OB/GYN, DENVER, CO

"Karen Hart has written a compelling story that explores the complexity of unintended teenage pregnancy in America today. She doesn't ignore the authenticity of young love or the power of the first blossom of passion. Though Ali Parker and her boyfriend Matt Ryan would both like to turn back time, the reality is that they must face the consequences of their actions and finally come to terms with what they feel is the 'right thing to do'—together and independently. Ms. Hart is well versed in adolescent development, and the push-pull of heart and mind is beautifully illustrated in her book as Ali Parker makes a critical decision about her future—one she makes with the tough and tender grace we see every day in our teenagers. Thankfully, they have access to public health and social services that offer the options they need to make difficult and very grown-up decisions. By reading *Butterflies in May*, we feel as if we've been at the family kitchen table for Ali's senior year in high school, and her journey into the adult world will resonate with both teenagers and parents alike."—MARY MARTHA WILSON, DIRECTOR OF TRAINING AND TECHNICAL ASSISTANCE, HEALTHY TEEN NETWORK (FORMERLY KNOWN AS THE NATIONAL ORGANIZATION ON ADOLESCENT PREGNANCY, PARENTING AND PREVENTION)

"Karen Hart's *Butterflies in May* is a gut-wrenching yet realistic look at teen pregnancy. Told in the first person, Ali's emotional, mental, and physical journey is a wonderfully accurate account that shows the far-reaching ripple effect that one 'mistake' can have. We as readers experience excellent character development in the reactions of the boyfriend, her parents, her friends, his parents, a trusted relative, teachers, and counselors. Often, teens naively think 'it's my baby, so it's my decision," but teen pregnancy forever changes so many lives. The reader's emotions will run the gamut as Ali explores her options—abortion, adoption, parenting. Perhaps there is the realization that once the threshold of teen sex is crossed, life's options change dramatically. This book is not only for girls, but also for boys and their families to read, and to frankly discuss 'what if' scenarios - the challenges and consequences of decisions before taking the leap into being sexually active. As Ali's mom points out, being well informed does not preclude our doing dumb things. I am haunted by a sad question that will always remain unanswered—what would Ali and Matt's future have been under different circumstances?"—DEBRA SMITH, HIGH SCHOOL TEACHER, LITTLETON, CO

"*Butterflies in May* is a touching story. I was moved by Hart's ability to convey the joy and heartbreak of a first love, the impossible number of emotions felt with unplanned pregnancy, and the very real teenage pressures of thinking about the future. Her story provides an over-the-shoulder glance at the reality of teenage pregnancy and the tough choices that go with it. I felt sympathy for both Ali and Matt as they were faced with this difficult situation, both unprepared for the hard choices they would have to make. Hart provides a wealth of information on the options and resources available to pregnant teens, as well as the advice that support is out there, and no one has to go through it alone."—AMY BRENINGER, SCIENCE TEACHER, MARIA CARRILLO HIGH SCHOOL, SANTA ROSA, CA

"*Butterflies in May* by Karen Hart is a story that chronicles a journey, taking a group of high school seniors along a winding path with unexpected obstacles and leading them into the realm of maturity. The book tackles the social taboo of teenage pregnancy with dignity, portraying the unsettling magnitude of premature adult responsibility. Ali Parker, the centerpiece of the novel, is seventeen and struggling to accept her situation of a predetermined future. She is forced into making choices that seem incomprehensible. The book focuses on how Ali arrives at her decisions, some that she will second-guess for many years, and provides insight into how her actions impact those around her, surprising even herself. Each character with whom she interacts is faced with typical adolescent problems, and each independently wrestles with choices that must be made to foster self-acceptance into adulthood. Karen Hart has written a story that responsibly teaches hard truths about the consequences of youthful impulse without imposing a verdict, providing an effective tool for pondering choices that adolescents rarely think will ever need their own personal consideration. She creates an avenue for empathetic understanding that immunity does not exist in life, but amnesty does."—NANCY BRODBECK, ASSISTANT PRINCIPAL, WARRENSBURG-LATHAM HIGH SCHOOL, WARRENSBURG, IL

"*Butterflies in May* is an incredibly appropriate book for high school students, as well as for adults. Reading it is a safe way for all such readers to experience and learn about often undiscussed topics. The physical, psychological, and emotional changes women go through during pregnancy were described perfectly. A variety of other extremely important subjects were also well dealt with: family, friendships, teen pregnancy, and high school love. Eventually, each was worked through, with the characters coming to terms with the most positive way to handle all situations."—KARA LEMKE, PHYSICAL EDUCATION TEACHER, MARIA CARRILLO HIGH SCHOOL, SANTA ROSA, CA